POPULAR

Other books in the
CANTERWOOD CREST SERIES:

TAKE THE REINS

CHASING BLUE

BEHIND THE BIT

TRIPLE FAULT

BEST ENEMIES

LITTLE WHITE LIES

RIVAL REVENGE

HOME SWEET DRAMA

CITY SECRETS

ELITE AMBITION

SCANDALS, RUMORS, LIES

UNFRIENDLY COMPETITION

CHOSEN

INITIATION

CANTERWOOD CREST

POPULAR

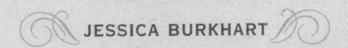 JESSICA BURKHART

ALADDIN M!X

New York London Toronto Sydney New Delhi

ALADDIN M!X

Simon & Schuster Children's Publishing Division

1230 Avenue of the Americas, New York, NY 10020

First Aladdin M!X edition May 2012

Copyright © 2012 by Jessica Burkhart

All rights reserved, including the right of reproduction
in whole or in part in any form.

ALADDIN is a trademark of Simon & Schuster, Inc., and related logo
is a registered trademark of Simon & Schuster, Inc.

ALADDIN M!X and related logo are registered trademarks
of Simon & Schuster, Inc.

For information about special discounts for bulk purchases,
please contact Simon & Schuster Special Sales
at 1-866-506-1949 or business@simonandschuster.com.

The Simon & Schuster Speakers Bureau can bring authors to your live event.

For more information or to book an event contact
the Simon & Schuster Speakers Bureau at 1-866-248-3049
or visit our website at www.simonspeakers.com.

Designed by Jessica Handelman

The text of this book was set in Venetian 301 BT.

Manufactured in the United States of America 0312 OFF

2 4 6 8 10 9 7 5 3 1

Library of Congress Control Number 2011940657

ISBN 978-1-4424-1950-6

ISBN 978-1-4424-1951-3 (eBook)

To Bri Ahearn

for being there in every way it counts (with kitty pics!)

and for listening!

ACKNOWLEDGMENTS

Popular wouldn't be in the hands of Team Canterwood members right now if it weren't for many people on Team Sparkle! Huge thanks to Simon & Schuster and everyone at Aladdin, especially Alyson Heller, Fiona Simpson, Bethany Buck, Dawn Ryan, Mara Anastas, Stephanie Voros, Carolyn Swerdloff, Jessica Handelman, Nicole Russo, Courtney Sanks, Deane Norton, Russell Gordon, Craig Adams, Karin Paprocki, Katherine Devendorf, Alex Penfold, Vanessa Williams, Lucille Rettino, and Liesa Abrams.

Monica Stevenson, thank you for snapping this gorgeous cover! To the New Era of Canterwood models and your families, thank you for being part of this journey. I couldn't have better faces for my characters. ☺

Team Canterwood, the outpouring of Go CCA! I receive from you via Facebook, Horse Mystique, Twitter, other forums, e-mail, and snail mail is *awesome* and humbling. I heart you all so much! You're the reason why Editor K and I work so hard on these books. We never want to disappoint you.

Speaking of Editor K . . . Kate Angelella, your purple pen gave this book so many popularity points. Thank you for the limitless effort you put into editing this book and shaping Lauren's story. As my best friend, you kept me going while writing with promises of *Homeland*, *The Real Housewives*, and Irish cheddar cheese. And cheese pasta. Your unwavering support keeps me going in more ways than you know. LYSSM. ♥

Ross Angelella, this is *your* year. I'm so proud and honored to have been able to witness the process of *Zombie* from all-nighters to ARCS. *Maybe* I'll watch a zombie flick with you . . . and annoy you like a little sister when I scream every five seconds.

A couple of random shout outs to T. C. Tweeps @: KayleyJOfficial, CanterwoodRider, horserider4567, jkrall07, and PaigeParkerXO. (If you're a CC fan who follows me, your handle could be in the next book!)

I wouldn't be sane without my friends: Lauren Barnholdt (I'm coming for your fireplace!), Brianna Ahearn (I wouldn't have Brittany S. Pierce without you!) and Andi, Becca Leach, Jennifer Rummel, Kelly Krysten, and Mandy Morgan.

Lexi and Grace C., big hugs! Happy riding!

Joey Carson, when are those plane tix to LA supposed to arrive, again? ☺

Thank you to all of the librarians and booksellers who have brought Canterwood to readers. And to the teachers who have been generous with allowing me to Skype with their students—I adore talking about writing and interacting with your talented, inquisitive students.

I

THE OLD,
THE NEW, AND THE
TOTALLY BUSTED

ALL FIVE FACES STARED AT ME. EACH GIRL'S expression was a variation of the girl before her.

Disbelief.

Confusion.

Shock.

Apprehension.

Curiosity.

Lexa.

Khloe.

Jill.

Clare.

Riley.

Seconds earlier, everything had slammed to a halt. The secret I'd been keeping for seven days—just one week, and my entire time at Canterwood Crest Academy—had been blown wide open.

A DVD I hadn't known existed had just outed me as "two-time junior dressage champion Lauren Towers." Or what I hadn't been able to explain yet—*ex* junior dressage champion.

The omission of my past experience with equestrian competition had been no accident. Now Jill, my new friend and Lexa's roommate, had innocently selected a DVD to watch while we all ate breakfast post-sleepover party. And bam: The DVD spilled the truth before I could even *think* about doing it myself.

"Yeah, right!" Riley balked. "This girl has *your* name, she *looks* like you, *and* when you heard the DVD in the background, you went white as an albino horse. And you expect us to believe you when you say that *isn't* you?"

Khloe's eyes bore into mine. Out of all the girls, I was closest to her. "Lauren," she said, glancing at the paused TV screen. "Even I have to agree. If you insist on denying that's you, it's going to be pretty much impossible to believe it."

"No, please—Khloe. I meant it—the girl on TV isn't me," I repeated. I glanced around, grateful that we were the only ones in Hawthorne Hall's common room.

Khloe, also my roommate, gripped the remote from when she'd paused the footage of the Red Oak Horse Trial. Khloe brushed a strand of blond hair from her face, her brown eyes looking from me to the floor.

I couldn't stand it if Khloe stayed mad at me. "Hear me out," I began.

Thunder rumbled over campus. Out of the corner of my eye, I saw a group of students bolt down the sidewalk, laughing, some trying to cover their heads with their backpacks.

The room darkened by the second. Lexa Reed, another seventh grader and my closest friend after Khloe, stood rigidly still. She tugged down her army green PJ tank that said SLEEP MONSTER on the front. She turned on a floor lamp. Once a warm yellow glow bathed the room in light, Lexa sat back down, pulling a blue chenille blanket over her dark caramel-colored legs.

No one spoke. It seemed as if none of us knew how to start.

The silence had gone on so long, it had turned everything to slow motion. I knew I had to be the one to say something.

"I'm sorry," I said. I cleared my raspy throat. "Please give me a chance to explain the DVD."

The other four girls looked at one another. It was as if they were getting each other's telepathic permission to let me speak.

Riley gathered her pin-straight black hair into a messy updo, secured with a clear band from her wrist. "Of course you can explain, Lauren." Her voice was sweeter than maple syrup.

"*I'm* listening," Clare added, blinking her blue eyes.

Lexa studied me for a second. Her curly black hair with natural reddish highlights hung around her face. Her jaw relaxed and her narrowed eyes softened. "I want to know too," she said, softer than the others.

All eyes went to Khloe. If she left, I didn't know what I'd do. She'd been more than my roommate—she'd been my best friend since I'd arrived on campus last week. But Khloe was quietest of all.

Her chest expanded as she took a deep breath.

I ran my tongue nervously over the permanent wire retainer along the back of my bottom teeth. It made me nauseous to think of losing Khloe as a friend just because I hadn't been able to bring myself to talk about my past—both my riding-circuit history and the big accident—to *anyone* yet. But I know it had been stupid to keep it a secret.

Finally, Khloe shrugged her shoulders, nodding a *yes*. Like the rest of us, she was still in pj's from last night. Her yellow tank and shorts with white polka dots had seemed so cheery then.

I shifted in my spot on the couch, opposite end from Khloe. No more secrets about my past on the A-circuit. I picked my cuticles, thinking back to *that* day.

New life, meet old life.

2

SECRET-SPILLING
SATURDAY

"LOOK—THAT GIRL?" I SAID. "SHE'S ME. BUT she's also not."

"Mystery solved, then!" Riley clapped, then rolled her eyes.

"Yes, I used to show competitively," I continued, ignoring her. "I rode for a bunch of different stables, and eventually I learned that dressage was my specialty."

The coffee pot beeped and the rich aroma of vanilla-flavored coffee filled the air. I craved a cup of tea—something calming like chamomile. But I didn't even know if *peppermint* tea—my de-stresser go-to—would settle my stomach this time.

I continued. "Two years ago, I was Lauren Towers—the

two-time national dressage champion. That—that title—it was everything to me."

Clare twisted wavy red strands of hair around her finger. Her face was full of questions, but I was prepared to answer every single one.

"If you're a 'two-time champion,'" Clare said, using air quotes, "then why are you on the *intermediate* team? Are you going to try and tell us that you were able to keep all this from Mr. Conner, too?"

"Of course not," I said. "He knows. But he judged my team placement solely on the test I did for him when I got here. Mr. Conner was upfront from the beginning. After my old coach told him about my competition history and"—I added, trying to hide my grimace—"Mr. Conner was very clear that my background would play zero role in his decision about what team I'd make. When I got here, he told me I'd be placed by my performance test—that it was the only fair way to do it. Based on my ride, he decided to place me with the advanced team."

"Did you agree with the way he judged you?" Lexa asked. Her tone was curious, not confrontational. "Or did you think he should have changed the rules and put you on the advanced team?"

Her question got Riley's attention. The other girl leaned forward from her spot on the couch opposite us, almond-shaped eyes widening.

"I agreed with him one hundred and ten percent. Believe it or not, I'm not ready for the pressure of the advanced team. Mr. Conner knew that. It took me a long, *long* time to even *ride* again after my accident." I paused. "I was . . . well, to be honest, I was terrified. For a long time, I thought I was done riding for good."

I let out a breath. I'd never said so much about the accident before, not ever.

Khloe still hadn't said a word. I hated that I couldn't figure out what she was thinking. I wished she'd say something—*anything*—just to give me a clue whether or not keeping such a big secret from her would trash our whole friendship. *Khlo,* I thought, wishing telepathy worked. *I wanted to tell you. I did. Please don't be mad.*

"So, like," started Jill, the only nonrider of all of us, "when did that accident happen?"

"Almost two years ago," I said, as evenly as possible. "I was competing at Red Oak on Skyblue—the gray on TV. He was a stable horse that I rode for Double Aces."

"That's right," Lexa said. "You *just* got Whisper. The accident's why you're riding a different horse, isn't it?"

"Kind of. I'd never owned a horse until Whisper. I picked her out, but she was a gift from my parents over the summer. A gift for getting into Canterwood." I pictured Whisper. Her light gray body, curly eyelashes, and white, pink, and black splotched muzzle. The vision of her sweet face was giving me strength for this extended Q & A session. I really liked most of the girls and, after we'd bonded during last night's sleepover, I really didn't want to lose any of them as friends just because I hadn't told them about my past as a competitive rider.

Last night, my first sleepover at Canterwood, had been *très parfait*. Khloe and I had invited the girls to our dorm for a Yay! We Survived Our First Week at Canterwood! night. We'd watched TV, played Truth or Dare, ate way too much candy—everything for a fun, perfect girls' night.

But in the morning, Khloe had suddenly received an e-mail from Canterwood's drama club advisor with news that she'd lost her dream role as Belle in the school's fall production of *Beauty and the Beast* to Riley, who also happened to be in the room.

Suffice to say, Riley was probably my least favorite of all the girls, and I knew she would not be likely to hide her glee about getting the role of Belle to spare Khloe's feelings. In fact, at the same time Khloe's eyes were welling with tears, Riley's face lit up with pride as Khloe read the e-mail to herself, then congratulated Riley.

We'd decided to turn this morning into a breakfast celebration of Khloe's role as Mrs. Potts—one of the best roles ever, we'd told her over and over—and albeit less enthusiastically Riley for her role as Belle. Jill came up with the fantastic idea to watch a horse show on DVD. It was the perfect diversion to keep Khloe's mind off Belle and to stop Riley from bragging her face off.

If I hadn't stayed to answer Mom's phone call, we might still be celebrating, I thought. Because in the five minutes I'd been on the phone, the girls had settled in the common room and Jill had chosen the Red Oak DVD I didn't even know existed.

As soon as I'd walked into the common room, I'd seen myself on TV. A girl with wavy brown hair who was crumpled on the ground. Pale skin looked stark against her black helmet. Her eyes were closed. Behind her, a dapple-gray horse—Skyblue—stood beside a vertical with faux greenery, looking worried that he'd injured his rider.

I shifted on the gray couch, my eyes now trained on Khloe but wanting to finally address the whole room to be sure they knew who I really was. I drew in a breath, composing myself. "You guys, I'm not this evil person with a ton of secrets. I had one—*had*—and Red Oak was it," I said. "I said I wasn't the person on TV because I'm *not*. Or, not anymore. That rider, the one onscreen"—my eyes flicked toward the TV—"she was focused on just one thing: winning. That's not me anymore.

"My parents gave up a lot and did everything they could so I could show and travel. So did my sisters. They moved to Union, where they still live, for me." My voice wavered. I couldn't even begin to count the endless sacrifices my family had made for me. "I'm lucky to be best friends with one of my sisters, but my relationship with my oldest sister is really damaged from having so much of my parents' attention."

"You did tell me you moved around a lot to show," Lexa said.

It felt like such a relief to hear someone else's voice other than my own. I smiled at her.

"That was true," I said. "But it would be more true to say that I had first place *locked* for both Double Aces and myself that day. But when I got to cross-country, I decided on course to finish fast even though my ride was clean and I was already well under time."

I glanced at Khloe. My roommate's arms, crossed only

minutes ago, were at her sides. Maybe she wasn't going to ask Christina, our dorm hall monitor, for a new roommate after all.

"Skyblue wasn't tired, so I pushed him toward the last jump," I said. "I was so confident we'd clear it and—to top it off—have a time that would impress everyone."

I grasped the pool-blue beryl stone on my necklace. It was a present from my parents—one I instinctively held whenever I got jittery.

"Adrenaline pumped through my body," I continued. "Skyblue moved so well under me. I still don't know for sure what happened. Maybe he gave me a hint that he was going to refuse the jump and I missed it. Or I did something wrong. I don't remember."

I stopped, lost in thought.

"Lauren?"

I blinked back tears and looked at Clare, who'd said my name. I hadn't noticed that she'd leaned forward from her spot next to Riley, her eyes wide. Khloe had lost her unaffected look; her lips weren't pressed in a firm line and her brown eyes were soft. But she stayed at her end of the couch.

"I'm sorry," I said. My voice was wobbly and thick. *Do not cry*, I told myself. I hated crying in front of people.

"It's, um"—I took a breath—"a little hard to talk about."

"You don't have to," Lexa said with a quiet and soothing tone.

I shook my head, swiping my hand across my eyes. "I want to. We're all starting to become friends. I'm *over* secrets. And if you guys are willing to listen, this is actually the first time I've *wanted* to talk about it."

The girls nodded. Outside the common room, Hawthorne residents had begun to wake and move around. I wanted to finish talking to my friends before more students joined us in the room.

"Skyblue and I moved toward the last jump," I said. "I remember thinking, 'I've got this. Easy.' But I was being arrogant. I was wrong. That jump—we didn't have it. Skyblue balked and I wasn't prepared. I sailed over the jump without him and slammed into the ground."

"Oh, Lauren," Jill said.

"Your parents must have been terrified," Riley said. She'd wrapped her arms around her legs, looking tiny in the oversized chair.

Riley had had one of her own secrets blown apart last night. We'd pushed her during what started out as a friendly game of Truth or Dare, and we'd accidentally made her cry. She'd told us about Toby, her younger brother with Down syndrome. Toby was the only soft spot perfect-slash-prickly Riley seemed to have.

"Were you injured?" Lexa asked.

I shook my head. "The hospital sent me home and told me to rest for a few days but to go ahead and ride when I wasn't sore from the fall."

"How long did you wait before riding?" Jill asked.

"I never rode Skyblue or another horse at Double Aces again," I said simply. "My mom got a job near Union, we moved there, and then . . ." I smiled. "I started to miss horses."

Everyone, even Jill, smiled. Some giggled. These girls knew what it was to miss riding the way I had. They really got it.

Lexa smiled. "Not easy to get them out of your blood, huh?"

"No." I laughed. "It did feel like it got inside my blood. I started to miss horses and riding about as much as I felt terrified at the thought of it. I learned how to ride all over again at Briar Creek. This time, as an *equestrian*. Not a ribbon collector."

"Did you compete there?" Riley asked.

"Not once," I said. "I was purely focused on letting go of my fears. Enjoying horses."

"How did you get from there to Canterwood?" Lexa asked.

With each question, it was getting easier to talk. It felt . . . *good*, in a weird way, to talk to my Canterwood friends about my past.

"Well, I rode there for a while. Then one day, my instructor brought up Canterwood. Even encouraged me to apply. She assured me that I was ready. And if I wanted to compete, Canterwood was the only place for me."

I shifted my gaze from face to face.

Khloe didn't look as cold toward me. Lexa's posture wasn't so rigid. Even the mood in general felt different— better—than when I'd started. I hoped I wasn't imagining it.

I pressed my dry lips together. "I'm sorry I lied to you all."

There was a pause, then the sound of someone clearing her throat.

Khloe.

"Well, ladies," she said. "What do we think?"

3

DEEPEST, DARKEST

SILENCE.

And more silence.

I looked from face to face. Still, no one answered her. I couldn't believe it! I'd ruined everything. My new friends thought of me as a liar and—

"Well, you did *lie* to us," Lexa said.

Riley, Clare, Jill, *and* Khloe nodded.

"And you *have* known us a week," Riley said.

Lexa, Clare, Jill, and Khloe nodded again.

I couldn't believe this. My first week and I'd already royally—

"A *week*," Clare repeated. "As if we'd expect you to spill your deepest, darkest secret in that amount of time!"

Wait, what?

Now everyone sported smiles—some even giggled.

"Lauren," Jill chimed in. "You *barely* know us. I get it. I would have been really, *really* scared to share something like that. It's pretty awesome of you to trust us the way you just did."

"Totally," Clare said, suddenly beside me. "But"—she slung an arm over my shoulder—"can you please breathe now? It's freaking us out." She shook me a little.

Relief rushed through me like liquid warmth spreading from head to toe. "Thank you, guys. I wasn't sure whether or not you'd judge me. I even wanted to tell you once." I looked at Khloe, wanting her to know I'd especially wanted to tell *her*. "But it's not the most fun thing to talk about in the whole world—the biggest mistake and most embarrassing moment rolled into one."

"Actually," Lexa said, "I'm sorry you had to keep that secret alone. But, trust me, we all have our Red Oak moments. I mean, Riley and Clare? They—"

"Are superprivate, too," Riley cut in, looking murderous. "And, like we said, a week is just not that long, when you think about it."

I nodded, glancing at a very pale Clare. Yikes—I had a feeling I wouldn't want to know *this* story for another couple of *hundred* weeks!

"I know that decision was mine, though, not to be upfront," I said.

"So that is that," Jill said firmly. She took off her black plastic-rimmed glasses and put them on the coffee table in front of her. "So . . . is this something you never want us to bring up again?"

"I actually don't mind," I said, surprised to hear the words coming out of my own mouth. "It gets easier every time I talk about it. And I want you all to feel like, if you want, you can ask any questions you have about any of it."

"*Well*, then . . . ," Lexa said, a sparkle in her eyes. "About the show circuit . . ."

"Lex!" Jill reached over and lightly punched her friend's knee. "Geez! Maybe Lauren, and the rest of us, could use a break for a minute or five. Say for, like, breakfast?"

"Oops. Sorry," Lexa said, smiling.

I smiled back. "I'm here whenever you need me. But now, breakfast, anyone?"

Riley stage-yawned. "Wish I could, ladies. But duty calls! I'm officially Belle now. I should dash so I can get the full script ASAP. Clare, let's go back to the room for our stuff so we can get to the theater? You know I need a partner to run lines. I'm sure there's, like, a *ton* of them."

That was the Riley I knew. "Officially Belle," as if the part had been hers all along. Like Mr. Barber, the drama advisor, allowed auditions as a mere *formality*.

Clare scratched her arm, looking between Khloe and Riley—both of them her BFFs. Clare was so soft-spoken and too nice to say no to a soul—let alone Riley. A fact that Riley was well aware of. I really did feel for sweet little Clare.

"If you go with Riley, could you pick me up a script?" Khloe asked Clare.

A look passed between them. Khloe understood and had just given Clare an out.

"Sure," Clare said, obviously relieved. She turned to me. "I'm sorry about the DVD, Lauren. But I'm glad you talked to us about it—now we get to know more about you."

"Thanks, Clare," I said.

Riley, waiting at the door, let out an exaggerated sigh. Clare hurried to her side. "Thanks for the fun sleepover," she said to Khloe and me as she ran after Riley.

"I'm having a serious coffee craving," Jill said. "Lex? Same?"

"You know me oh so well, roomie," Lexa said. "Let's caffeinate ourselves, girls."

The four of us walked over to the common room's kitchen and Jill handed each of us a mug. Mine was white with lilac hearts.

I went ahead and filled the stainless-steel teakettle and put it on the stove, waiting for boiling water.

"Tea?" I asked Khloe, without even thinking. It had become somewhat of a habit to offer Khloe tea whenever I got my own.

Khloe put her back to the counter and hopped onto it, scooting back and next to a bowl of bananas, apples, and plums. "Tea sounds perfect." She shot me a smile.

I felt very proud. Coffee had been Khloe's first love, but in just one week I'd gotten her hooked on tea. I just had to tell her that tea had even more caffeine than coffee sometimes—*and* it came in a ton of yummy flavors.

Jill and Lexa made their coffees—Lexa's mug was filled with more milk and sugar than actual coffee.

Once the teakettle whistled, I poured the steaming water into Khloe's mug, then mine. I reached into the cabinet where I'd stored my tea stash and held Khloe's mug out to her. She plucked a packet of Bigelow French Vanilla and a Splenda from the basket.

"Thanks," she said.

I peered at her sneakily. Had it been my imagination,

or did she sound sort of . . . standoffish? I had to talk to Khloe alone. ASAP. Her one-word response rattled around in my brain while I dropped a bag of Celestial Seasonings Chamomile into my mug. Was it possible that she really wasn't okay about the DVD? Khloe was an actress, after all. Maybe she didn't want the other girls to know, but she was really seriously hurt and disappointed that I, her roommate, had lied to her. *Oh, no.*

I put away the tea basket, remembering my Splenda only after I had closed the cabinet door. I didn't go back for it. Khloe stayed on the counter, which was in the middle of the kitchen. I blew on my tea across from her next to the stove.

Lexa and Jill grabbed two cheese pastries and put them on pink napkins. Were they sneaking glances at Khloe and me?

"Oh, shoot, Jill," Lexa said. "I totally forgot that I have a paper to write this morning. I need books from the library . . . and there's *no* way I can carry them all. Want to eat breakfast while we get our stuff from KK and Laur's room?"

Okay, now I knew something was up. *Shoot?* A paper to write *Saturday morning?*

"Sure," Jill said. "We'll catch up with you guys later.

Promise me you'll do something more exciting than going to the library for research books!"

Neither Khloe nor I called Jill and Lex on their obvious library lie. They left, and a second later the door opened. A couple of girls I sort of recognized walked inside.

"Hey, Lauren!" one of the girls, a petite brunette, said. The girl next to her smiled, showing braces with blue bands. "Hi, Khloe!"

"Hi," I said.

Khloe smiled at them. The girls chatted with each other while pouring bowls of Lucky Charms.

I looked at Khloe tentatively. "Want to take breakfast back to our room?"

She nodded. "Let's."

I was too nervous that Khloe might hate me to be hungry. I grabbed a blueberry muffin and my tea while Khloe did the same—only she took a cranberry scone. We sidestepped Hawthorne Hall dorm mates as doors opened and girls flooded into the hallway, going up and down the stairs in fuzzy slippers, socks, and bare feet.

Khloe opened the door to our room and I followed her inside. Everyone's sleeping bags and clothes were gone. Remnants of last night—nail polish, Japanese candy wrappers, and DVD boxes—were strewn everywhere.

I shut the door and tried to wait for Khloe to speak first, but I couldn't keep it in a second longer. I started talking without even putting down my tea and breakfast.

"Okay," I said. "You've barely said one word to me since we left this room. Please say something. Do you want a new roommate or something?"

Khloe slowly put her mug and scone down on her desk. "Maybe I do."

4

NOW TELL ME HOW
YOU REALLY FEEL

YES, I'D ASKED THE QUESTION. BUT I HADN'T
been prepared for *that* answer.

Drops of scalding tea splashed over the side of my mug
as I put it down with a trembling hand. "You do?"

"Yup," Khloe said, her voice and face emotionless. "I
totally hate you, Lauren, and I never want to speak to you
again."

My feet felt as though they'd been cemented to the
floor. I was too stunned to even process what she'd said.
My mouth dropped open.

"LT!" Khloe ran up to me and gripped my forearms. "You
know me better than that! I'm not going to stop being your
friend or roommate because of what you told us." She pulled
me into a hug, then let me go so she could see my face.

I sucked in a breath so hard, it made me cough. *Oh, mon Dieu!* Actress Khloe *seriously* had to work on her timing!

"You. Scared. Me," I said, letting myself freak out the way I'd wanted to two minutes ago. "You looked a thousand percent serious in the common room. I thought I'd lost my first and closest Canterwood friend."

Khloe took my hand and led me to her bed. We sat cross-legged on her crumpled zebra-print sheets, facing each other. "I'm so sorry!" Khloe said, cringing. "I need to be a *teensy* bit more sensitive about the acting thing. Note to self: not the right time to try my I-can-do-without-you-and-don't-even-care character."

I rubbed my forehead, wanting to shake Khloe. But I was too relieved that she didn't really hate me. "Khlo, I want you to know something. As much as it's going to sound like a convenient coincidence, I really *was* going to tell you today. You've been an amazing friend to me—I knew I could talk to you about Red Oak. I wanted to talk to you first."

"I buy it." Khloe nodded. "It doesn't sound like a cover. Plus, I *am* totally trustworthy."

"I don't know." I laughed. "I might need to rethink that one."

Khloe stuck out her bottom lip and batted her lashes in a giant pout.

"Oh, *please*," I said. "But seriously, Khlo—how *do* you feel about everything? I really want to know."

Khloe pulled her blond hair over one shoulder. "I'm glad you don't have to hide it anymore. I understand why you did—I do. If we'd been roommates for, like, *years* and then you decided to tell me, it would be a little different, you know? But it's been a week."

"I didn't hurt your feelings?" I asked.

"Not at all," Khloe said, pausing for a half second. "I'm honored you wanted to tell me first. Who knew Jill was going to pick *that* DVD? Hello, complete fluke."

"I know!" I said, shaking my head. "I really wish it hadn't come out like that."

Khloe reached for her scone, broke off a piece, and offered it to me. "But at least now it's over. No more secrets. That has to feel good, right?"

"You know what? It does," I said. "I think I'm maybe still in shock, though, too. We went from sleepover to . . . well, *that* in less than ten seconds."

"Oh—I know—go get your tea," Khloe said. "I know you, LT, and you need some tea to calm you down."

I smiled in agreement, then got up to get my mug and breakfast plate. With my back to Khloe, I took a breath. Ninety-nine point nine percent of me believed every word

Khloe had said—but I wanted to give it more time. Her feelings were *incredibly* important to me.

I sat on my own bed, setting everything on my night-stand. I took a gulp of the now-lukewarm tea and looked at Khloe.

"I've got fifty million questions!" Khloe said. "The only reason you're going to regret telling me is because I'm going to drive you crazy with all of them."

"And we've got all day," I said. The dramatics were *very* Khloe Kinsella. I was happy to see something familiar about my crazy roommate. "Ask me anything."

Her scone now devoured, Khloe fluffed her pillow and settled back, looking as if she was taking my "all day" comment quite literally.

"How long were you on the show circuit? No, wait—how'd you even get started?" Khloe asked.

"I rode a pony at a birthday party when I was five," I said. "And, done—I was totally hooked on horses. My mom talks about that party to this day. She claims that I asked if we could tie one of the ponies behind the car and take it home."

Khloe laughed. It was the same happy laugh I'd heard a lot last week. "I would have probably done the same."

"Then I pestered my parents until they let me take

lessons. They finally enrolled me in beginner classes at Winding Road Stables. It was really close to our house in Syracuse, New York, where I was born. I'm sure my asking five times a day to ride played *some* part in their decision."

"Nah, parents *love* it when their kids ask for the same thing on repeat," Khloe teased.

I smiled, thinking of my first stable. "It didn't take me long to move up the ranks at Winding Road. I started competing at six and there was no going back. Early on, I showed every few months. As I got older and more experienced, the times between competitions got shorter and shorter. My instructor told my parents that I needed to go beyond regional competitions—start competing around the country."

"Wow," Khloe said. "How did you feel about leaving home?"

"Excited, mostly," I said. "All of my friends were riders. Plus, I knew my dad would go with me anywhere I went."

"How?" Khloe asked.

"He's a writer," I said. "As long as he had his laptop, he could go anywhere. Mom stayed home with Becca and Charlotte. Sometimes, if she had a free weekend and I wasn't too far away, she'd bring my sisters. We'd run around the hotel and swim."

Khloe reached over and stopped her vibrating phone. "Wow, you have an amazing family. I know you have some stuff with Charlotte, but it's incredible your parents and Becca were so cool with traveling and everything that comes with being on the circuit."

"I really do love my family," I agreed. "My parents did *everything* they could in order for me to pursue my dreams. Becca *is* the best sister. She never resented me for taking Mom or Dad away from home so they could chaperone me. She even got *Charlotte* excited when we moved to Union. She always tried to make Char understand how Mom and Dad would do for either of them what they did for me."

"So Union was after Brooklyn and Red Oak. What did you do?" Khloe asked. "I mean, was never riding again a serious consideration, like you said?"

"Oh, are you kidding? I was very serious about that. Like I told you guys in the common room, I thought I was done for *good* after the accident. It was *awful*. Even the thought terrified me. I couldn't imagine ever getting into the saddle again." I paused, twisting the white-gold ring with a horseshoe made of tiny diamonds around my pointer finger. "It wasn't so much about falling or being afraid of getting hurt. It was the shock—I didn't have any clue *how* the accident had even happened! Now, of course, I see it clearly—it was my ego. I could have *really* hurt Skyblue. But I was *so* set on winning. I wasn't focused on him the way I should have been. That must have been the reason I made a big mistake."

Khloe opened her nightstand drawer, pulled out a tube of Urban Decay gloss, and ran it over her lips.

"When I saw the DVD," she said, "I wasn't a thousand percent focused trying to see whose fault the accident was, but I don't think you made a mistake. Or, not an obvious one, anyway. No horses are bomb proof; you and I know that. You can't be sure it *wasn't* Skyblue."

I got up to make another cup of tea in our microwave. "I know. I'll never be one hundred percent sure. I've had to accept it and try not to go back and figure it out. I did the whole was-it-me-or-was-it-not thing for a while, and it drove me insane."

"The move sounds like it was good for all of you. Total fresh start," Khloe said.

"It was exactly that. I missed Brooklyn a lot at first— when I want sushi at midnight or a one-block walk to the coolest shops ever. But moving to Union was the best thing that could have happened to me and my family, Khloe."

"Which, if I'm not mistaken, is how you ended up at the famous Briar Creek—former home of the Youth Equestrian National Team hotness, Miss Sasha Silver."

Just hearing Sasha's name made me pumped to go back to riding lessons. *I* wanted to be the girl from Union that made it too. Maybe some girl would drool over my riding someday, the way Khlo and I fawned over Sasha's.

"Exactly." I nodded, punching buttons on the microwave. "The instructor there, Kim, worked her magic on me. She took every lesson slow, knowing what had happened. I realized my biggest problem pretty quickly—I'd forgotten the most important thing: to love horses before even caring about competition. I fell in love with horses all over again at Briar Creek. I took lessons, didn't show, and made friends who loved horses."

Khloe smiled. "I know this one! Brielle and Ana, right?"

"Very good! They were the first people to reach out to me at Briar Creek. The three of us had an insta-bond. We were inseparable at school, too."

"Well, if they're *your* friends, I *know* they're awesome," Khloe said, giggling. "We'll have to pretend they're your sisters or something, so we can get them here for Family Day!"

"Well, the names of 'two sisters' were left off my application."

We both laughed.

"Seriously, though, I don't want to spend all day grilling you," Khloe said. "I'm really just curious."

"Oh, I know! And I'm not uncomfortable. I promise. I *want* to tell you all this stuff. You're my closest friend *and* my roommate."

The microwave beeped. I took my hot water out and sneaked a glance at Khloe while choosing my tea. There was something *off* still. But I didn't know what.

Maybe she was just processing everything I'd told her. Maybe she really was a little hurt, mad, or both. Or maybe I was overthinking it.

I dropped a cinnamon apple tea bag into my mug, turning around.

Khloe smiled at me—the playful *you're so gullible* smile she'd given me so many times since we'd met. "C'mon, LT," she said. "I'm totally using the Q & A sesh as an acting exercise in case I get cast as the next Cat Love, the reporter for *Celeb Roundup* on the Watch! channel. Or if I'm hired to do one of those prime-time hour-long backstage gigs with singers on *Voice It!* before America decides whether to kick them off or keep them on. And I'm the one that would be all, 'to vote DJ Disco Pop, chat us up at Chatter slash *Voice It* dot com. Don't forget to hash tag DJDP!' I'll be so prepped for this!"

And just like that, my fears evaporated.

What had I been thinking?

If Khloe Kinsella was upset, she'd tell me. No doubt about it—Khloe didn't keep anything from anyone. Particularly her own annoyance.

I grinned. "So glad I could be of service."

5

GENIUS FREAK,
THE BOY MAGNET

KHLOE GOT UP AND GRABBED A DIET COKE
from our mini fridge. She opened it, stuck a royal blue
straw in the can, and sat on her bed, facing me. "I guess
there's just one . . . ," she started. She opened and closed
her mouth a couple of times before closing it all together.

"Khlo," I said. "You can ask me *anything*. I want more
than anything for you to feel like you have answers to
your questions. Please feel free to bring it up anytime if
you think of anything at all."

Khloe nodded slowly. "Well, so . . . were you really
scared about testing for the riding team or was that was
an act? You obviously have the experience. Was that you
trying to fit in or was it real?"

"If I can promise you anything, it's that all of that was

real," I said. "I was *terrified* about testing. There were so many components that went along with whatever team I made. Sometimes I didn't even know which one I wanted."

Khloe cocked her head. "What do you mean?"

"Well, if I made the beginner team, I could keep working on basics with *zero* pressure to show. I'd be completely comfortable. It would be like I could start with a safety net and test later for intermediate. But if I made the intermediate team right away, I'd be taking lessons with riders I *knew* were most likely focused on competition and probably had their hopes up that they'd make the advanced team. There would also be more showing with the intermediate team."

"I think that's where I get a little lost," Khloe said.

"What do you mean?" I asked.

Khloe looked at me dead-on. "Lauren. You have *two* national titles. Your experience alone should qualify you for the advanced team. The accident *really* shook your confidence. I mean, enough to even make you consider the beginner team. Do you get how much better you are than that?"

"The accident changed everything I thought I knew about riding," I said. "So, yes. I get how much it shook me. Logically, I know people fall all of the time. But that accident turned me totally upside down. Being afraid of horses is a beginner-level fear. So to me, it made sense I'd have a chance of landing a spot on the *beginner team*."

"And are you completely happy with Mr. Conner's decision?" Khloe asked. "I know you said you were, but you were also in front of Riley and everyone when you said that. I wanted to ask you alone. Just you and me. *Are* you happy about Mr. Conner's decision?"

"I *am* happy where he placed me. It was time to step up and not be stagnant. I'm going to compete when I feel ready. Until then, I feel lucky to have Mr. Conner teaching Whisper and me."

Khloe nodded. "Fair enough. And look, I don't mean to drag this convo out more, but I have to say, I'm still adjusting to knowing this part of you. Everything I thought I knew about you—from your relationships with Charlotte and Becca to the real meaning of you finding Whisper . . . it all sort of revolves around something I didn't know before."

My shoulders slumped a little.

"But," she added quickly, "I'm honored to know you even better now. Everything we've talked about gives me a clearer sense of *you* than before. Some things even have *more* meaning behind them now. It's not like a mad thing at *all*; I'm not mad, I promise. I'm just, you know, digesting."

Khloe looked at me, but I turned quickly to hide the downcast expression on my face. Still, the sudden movement must have signaled alarm bells to her.

"LT. You are still *Lauren Towers*: new girl on campus, roomie to Khloe Kinsella, owner of the stunningly beautiful Whisper, intermediate riding team member, boy *magnet*, genius freak taking a crazy amount of classes—have you realized the error of your ways yet, by the—no? Okay, then, last, glee club member."

Her words—and theatrics, of course—made me smile.

"Genius freak?" I parroted back at her in mock disdain.

"And boy magnet, but we're losing focus, LT. And the focus is this: *Nothing* you told me today has changed who you are."

It was exactly what I *hoped* she'd say. "Khlo!" I said. "I'm *so* glad you're my friend. Truth? I'd have been crushed if I'd lost even a drop of our friendship."

Khloe took a sip of soda, then smiled. "Me too, LT. We're cool like that—you know why? Because I feel the same way. And as your friend, I wish you a speedy recovery from this morning. It probably felt like someone dropped a Canterwood handbook on top of your head when you saw that DVD. Welcome to Riley's world," she snorted. "We'll get her back, though."

"Those handbooks do weigh a ton," I said with a wry smile. Then it hit me like two more handbooks. "Wait—what?"

But Khloe was still going. "Thing is, you took it all in stride—OMG, and with such grace! I wouldn't have been as cool as you. I'm sorry everything happened the way it did, but I'm glad to know more about pre-Canterwood Lauren. Plus, my roomie is a dressage champ and I can, like, *make* her practice with me."

I laughed briefly. "You're helping *me*, remember? But about Riley—"

Khloe wagged a blue-black polished finger at me. "Do *not* waste one second on that girl. We will get her . . . my pretty."

We smiled at each other. I was still unsure how to decode the Riley factor, but Khloe's eyes went directly to the plasma TV. "Besides, it's Saturday. Only the most awesome day invented. Especially for students attending schools like Canterwood, where teachers give us enough homework that we're essentially reduced to tears every Friday."

"Tears. Yes. Following you," I said, though I was sort

of just half following, half trying to figure out what direction we were going in. But I'd learned to ask what I referred to in my mind as "clarity questions." So, sure, I could tell her I was following her. Then I'd ask a clarity question, such as, "What exactly do you have in mind?"

"Reality TV. Prime-time soapy dramas. Movies. Ordering in. Any of that sound good to you?"

Et voilà. Clarity.

"Only everything!" I said, meaning every word. "Let's do it!"

For the rest of the day, Khloe and I flipped channels together, deciding what to watch and laughing at each other's commentary on why or why not to watch a show.

Slowly, the tightness in my chest that had settled over me in the morning expanded, released, and eventually went away.

Altogether, Old Lauren was gone for good. In her place was Lauren 2.0. Lauren, the Genius Freak Boy Magnet whose BFF was all about the drama, knew 2.0's deep, dark secrets, and, in the end, loved 2.0 all the more for them.

6

1 FRESH HAYBALE
1 PINCH CINNAMON
PREPARE TO SWOON

MONDAY AFTERNOON, I HEADED TOWARD THE
stable after class.

Usually I sprinted down the sidewalk to reach the stable
as fast as possible.

However, today's sprint was replaced by scuff-dragging
my boots along the concrete. I couldn't walk any slower—
trust me, I'd tried. I wished for the ability to become
invisible. Of all days to wish for such a power—I wanted
it most now. I could bypass all of the other riders and
huddle next to Whisper in her stall. I'd tell her all about
what had happened on Saturday.

Khloe and I had stayed up late Saturday night, giggling over bad romantic comedies, which led to the inevi-
table "who's hottest in Hollywood conversation" We

discovered we had *very* similar taste in guys. Outgoing, funny, athletic. And we both loved blue eyes. The following day—Sunday—had been quiet. We'd intermittently done homework and watched TV together.

Finally, I approached the stable's main entrance. I hadn't spoken to Cole or Drew about Secret-Spill Saturday. Yesterday, Lexa had BBMed me asking if I wanted her to tell Cole what the girls had found out. Since Lexa and Cole were besties, I'd gladly said *yes*. Lexa once told me—with Cole's permission, of course—that he'd been through struggles of his own before Canterwood, his much more serious than mine. He'd been so cool about sharing his past with me; I knew he'd be cool about mine.

True to character, Lexa had met up with me before our first class together and told me that of course Cole understood why I'd kept my secret.

That left Drew as the last one on our intermediate team to know about Red Oak. Unless, of course, Riley had told him. And, according to the monologue that Khloe had performed for me on Sunday afternoon, planting the Red Oak DVD and getting Jill to play it was the least of what Riley was capable of. Khloe had been oddly secretive about what, exactly, Riley had done that was so . . . awful. Nor was she forthcoming about why she thought Riley was to blame for Saturday's Secret Spillage. Still, she insisted that Riley was capable of anything and, even though Riley had surprised me with her reaction Saturday morning, I still didn't trust her. And no matter how many details Khloe left out of her story, I trusted my roommate more than any other girl on campus.

I stood outside the stable's wide entrance—frozen—as horses and riders moved inside. Shod hooves clinked down the main aisle, and riders called out to one another. *What's your problem?! Go or you'll be late!* I yelled at myself. Still, I couldn't make myself step inside.

"I know you're new and everything—but, uh, you *do* know that you have to go inside to find your horse, don't you?"

I jumped, turning to see Drew beside me, grinning. Sunlight glinted off his black hair; his pale skin contrasted against his coffee brown polo shirt and matching breeches.

"I . . ." I trailed off, brilliantly.

This was *exactly* what I'd been afraid of—or *whom*, I guess.

Drew.

I hadn't seen him at all today. He'd been excused from gym for some reason, so we hadn't been able to talk at all.

"Drew—"

"—Lauren . . ."

We both laughed at our verbal collision.

"You first," I said, like a big chicken.

"You sure?" he asked politely.

I nodded fervently, my head bobbing like a chicken's!

"Lauren," Drew said. "I just wanted to say, you don't have to talk about . . . um, your accident. Riley actually explained everything."

Suddenly, the absence of noise felt deafeningly loud.

"Drew," I said, looking into his eyes. I was pleased to hear that my voice sounded stronger to me. Khloe would have been proud. "I'm so sorry you heard that from Riley. But not because I didn't want you to know." My eyes darted across Drew's face—his deep-ocean-blue eyes were soft as they settled on me. He looked curious—like he couldn't wait to hear what I'd say next.

I smiled at him, testing the waters. He smiled back, and I felt myself go soft in the knees.

"Well," I said. "I was hoping to use it as an excuse to talk to you. Like, at The Sweet Shoppe or something, sometime?"

Gasp! Had those words really come out of *my* mouth?

Somewhere on campus, Khloe was playing with a Lauren

Towers look-alike doll with long dark hair, caramel colored breeches, and a white-and-purple striped button-down.

Drew's smile was spread wide across his face—his bright white teeth peeking out from under his lips. "Riley did tell me a little, but I'd be more inclined to hear the story from the person who actually speaks from experience. See, Riley said it took you a while to start riding again."

"But I was just going to say that I—" I started, feeling defensive.

"No, no," Drew cut in, holding up his hands. I noticed the calluses on his palms from the reins. "I think it's brave that you got back to doing what you love."

I stared at him, blinking. This guy was amazing. He didn't even know me, and here he was, telling me how brave he thought I was.

Ironically, it was one of the bravest things a boy had ever said to me.

"I hope you're not embarrassed," Drew said, breaking our silence. "I mean, I'm a jumper so . . . my falls are pretty epic." He laughed.

His voice was much deeper than those of the other guys in our grade. I figured he probably would sing baritone in glee.

Snap out of it! I told myself.

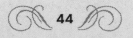

Drew stood across from me.

And, I reminded myself, *he just informed you that Riley, of all people, told him your deepest, darkest secret.*

How.

Humiliating.

My cheeks felt as though they'd glow in the dark. I thought how amazing that invisibility thingy would be about now.

It was then that I heard a voice much more powerful than my own, or Drew's, or even Mr. Conner's. It was Khloe's voice in my head, furious that I was letting Riley win like this.

"Wow," I said. "Thank you for saying that. No one had ever said that to me before. Maybe because it wasn't 'bravery' so much as an addiction to riding."

"But you didn't quit. You took a break, right?"

I nodded.

"Well, that was smart," Drew said. "Gave you the distance you needed before starting back up again. And, Laur, I've watched you during lessons. You're a talented rider." He leaned closer to me. He was close enough to smell like fresh hay and cinnamon mints. "What a waste of talent that would have been," he said, his eyes twinkling, "if you really *had* quit."

I opened my mouth to respond, but the words never came out. It wasn't like me to be shy around guys! But Drew's compliment, coupled with the cozy warmth of his scent and the way my name sounded in his mouth, made me positively dizzy.

"Drew! C'mon!" Before I could speak, a tall, unfamiliar-looking redheaded guy clapped Drew on the back of his shoulder and tilted his chin in the direction of the stable.

Drew shot me a dazzling smile and started forward. "See you, Lauren." He followed the guy, then turned back. "If you ever *do* want to tell me that whole story sometime, you know where I'll be."

I shook my head, making a face I wasn't used to making—impressed. "But," I said, ready to lead with the foot I always stepped with first, "last one to finish warming up buys."

Drew looked puzzled. "We're not even tacked up yet," he said, incredulous.

"Sounds like you should beat me easy, then." I laughed.

7

FIVE HUNDRED
AND FOUR

I COULDN'T GET THE SMILE OFF MY FACE while I groomed and tacked up Whisper. I'd *promised* myself before school started that I would focus on just two things: school and riding. But I couldn't help it. There was something . . . magnetic about Drew. Besides, Khloe would kick my butt if she caught me choosing my GPA over a guy like Drew.

I leaned close to Whisper, stroking her neck. "Drew's a good rider, girl. We could swap advice or something. Then, technically, no rules would be broken."

Whisper craned her neck, her big brown eyes on mine. Her expression was identical to the one Becca would have given me if I'd fed her that exception to my own lame rule.

"Let's see if we beat him, Wisp," I said.

But up ahead, a silky black tail swished as a blonde fumbled with her girth's buckles.

"Khlo?" I led Whisper next to Ever and halted her.

Khloe's fair face—not just her cheeks—was flushed. She looked kind of dazed but had a sort of perma-smile over her lips.

"What's . . . ? You okay?"

"No!" Khloe replied. "Yes! I don't know!"

"What's going *on*?" I asked, leading Whisper closer to her and Ever, out of the way of the main aisle.

Khloe looked down the aisle at the wall clock. "I'll make you late. You need to be in the arena right now. Argh! I want to talk now, though!"

Drew was going to win, that I knew. On the other hand, I had to know what was up with Khloe.

"Then I'll be late," I said. "There's no way I'm going to my lesson without finding out what's going on."

"Okay! Omigod, Laur!" Khloe practically pounced on me. She was inches from my face as she bounced on her toes. Ever eyed her—likely trying to process Khloe's erratic behavior. "I'll be really quick. I promise on—"

"Spill it!" I said, shaking my head and laughing.

"It was Zack. We ran into each other on our way to the stable and talked the entire way here!"

"Khlo!"

"Get this—he actually *liked* the text photo you guys made me send during Truth or Dare! He thought it was funny and that it was 'cute.'" She giggled, using air quotes. "He liked that I went through with the dare."

"See! And you were afraid that picture would *ruin* your social life."

"I know!" Khloe shook her head. "When we got to the tack room? He *opened* the *door* for me! We took *way* too long in there. And . . . ," Khloe trailed off, her grin growing.

"Aaand?" I asked.

"Zack asked if I wanted to go out and hit up The Slice with him sometime!" Khloe's glossy pink smile couldn't have been any wider.

"Khlo! That's amazing!" I grabbed her in a hug and we rocked back and forth, squealing when necessary. Whisper and Ever stood together quietly, heads down and eyes shut, as if they were just too embarrassed of their boy-crazy owners.

Various riders who passed our tiny freak-out barely batted an eye at us. They all just kept moving as if Khloe and I just happened to be doing normal stable chores. Finally, one rider stopped.

"Did someone get good news?" Riley cooed. "Aw!" Her finger oscillated between me and Khloe before settling on Khloe like the Wheel of Fortune needle (or in this case— *misfortune*). "Khloe, I bet it's you! Did Ever finally take the ditch? I saw her balk at it a couple of days ago."

Khloe's face went from being flushed with happiness to blotchy, angry red. "Something happened that I'm sharing with my *friend*," Khloe said, glaring at Riley. The other girl didn't budge. I looked from one to the other. Riley was beyond stubborn.

But Khloe had it *out* for that girl lately, so no way would she give in either. If no one made a move soon, we'd be standing here staring at one other until the outdoor lights came on. Or Mr. Conner kicked us out. Whichever came first.

Khloe tossed her blond hair, giving Riley a gigantic smile. "Well, you certainly don't seem to have anywhere to go . . . or, for that matter, anyone to see . . ."

Riley leaned closer. It was short-lived, but I could have sworn I'd seen a hurt—maybe even surprised—look cross her face. Quickly enough, Riley's cool, indifferent mask covered her face again. "Actually, if you could *not* take forever? Clare's waiting by the arena with Adonis."

Khloe made an exaggerated *O* with her mouth. "Oh, well, never mind, then! I wouldn't want *you* to be late, precious."

Riley's mouth opened and closed, guppielike. Poor thing wanted to know our gossip so much, I half expected her to stand on her tiptoes, clap her arms together, and start barking like a seal.

I almost felt sorry for her.

"Okay. I'm not saying a thing," I taunted. "But if I said anything, I'd just *mention* that Khloe is most likely, almost for sure, soon to . . . mmm . . . very soon, probably be off the market," I cut in.

I said I *almost* felt sorry for Riley.

"Byeee!" I said to Khloe. "Talk to you in our room later. I want to hear *every* detail."

Khloe and I traded *ha!* looks before I led Whisper down the aisle.

Riley stayed a few feet behind us, her boots clomping against the ground louder than Whisper's hooves.

Clare, waiting at the indoor arena entrance, held her own horse, Fuego, and Adonis. She smiled at me, but it faded when Riley snatched Adonis's reins from her hand and didn't say a word. Clare pulled her black helmet down further over her forehead, whispering "hi" to me as she followed Riley inside.

I mounted Whisper and looked around. Drew, Cole, and Lexa were already warming up their horses. Riley,

Clare, and I had been the last ones to arrive.

I trotted Whisper up to Drew. "When did you get here?" I teased. "I've been here forever."

He laughed—a deep, genuine laugh. "Strange, I was wondering where *you* were. I'm sure we were too wrapped up in practicing to notice each other."

"That, *and* this arena"—I swept my arm in an arc—"is huge. So easy to miss each other."

Drew and I laughed together.

"Drew?"

Our gaze broke. Riley, sitting tall in Adonis's saddle, smiled angelically. She'd just *appeared*—like she'd some-how made Adonis tiptoe over.

"What's up?" he asked.

"I'm *so* sorry to interrupt you guys," Riley said. She made an apologetic face. "Drew, I can catch you later."

Riley pulled on Adonis's left rein to turn him away.

"You're not interrupting," I said. The second the words left my mouth, Riley reined Adonis to face us.

"Drew, I know you're crazy busy with swimming and everything, but would you have a second this week to help me with our class's science paper? I have an idea for the subject, but I'm *sure* it's bad."

Riley made a frowny-slash-sad face. I looked away

from her, focusing on Drew. I hadn't even known he was a swimmer. His pale skin and lack of chlorine smell hadn't given the slightest hint. It would give us something else to talk about. I knew a lot about the sport from being with Taylor.

"No prob," Drew said. "Text me or something, and we'll go over it."

Riley shot me a *blink and you'll miss it* smug smile. "Thanks, Drew!" she chirped.

"We better start warming up or we'll be mucking stalls together," Drew said. The three of us moved our horses along the wall, joining Clare, Lexa, and Cole. Each of us kept our horses spaced out—no tailgating—and moved through a smooth warm-up. My attention was fully on Whisper, and as I posted, it felt as if nothing else existed. The only sounds I heard were her hoofbeats and breath.

I looked up—startled—to see Mr. Conner standing in the arena's center, watching us. No one had moved to stop.

"Exactly what I've been hoping to see," Mr. Conner called. "Come to the center."

I eased Wisp to a walk and rode beside Lexa and Cole to halt in front of Mr. Conner.

"Not one of you stopped when I came into the arena,"

Mr. Conner said, his smile reaching his brown eyes. "Each of you had great focus, and it was the most fluid, together session I've seen from this group. I hope to see more of this in the future—you treating practice as important as the actual lesson."

We traded smiles with each other. Mike and Doug, two of the stable hands, carried plastic poles under each arm, and began creating a cavaletti course. They stacked wooden holders along the wall and laid poles on the ground, measuring the space with yellow measuring tape.

"I was going to wait until the lesson was over to discuss some important news with you," Mr. Conner said. "However, based on what I just witnessed, I think now is the right time to talk."

I glanced over at Lexa, then Cole, forgetting about the cavaletti. Both had the same expression: no clue what Mr. Conner was about to say. I gripped the reins a little tighter. It surely wouldn't be *bad* news . . . would it?

"As you're all aware, this is the start of your second week at Canterwood," Mr. Conner said. "We're just beginning the season and getting used to lessons and riding on a regular schedule. Soon it will be time to ease into the competition circuit."

I took a sharp breath, almost making myself cough. If

any of my teammates noticed, they didn't react. Lexa and Cole leaned forward to see around me and grinned at each other. In the mirror, I saw Drew high-five Cole. Clare and Riley had matching grins.

Flashes of past competitions—wins and losses—blinked in front of me. Part of me couldn't wait to compete on *my* horse and show the judges what beautiful moves Whisper possessed. The other part wanted to gallop Whisper out of the arena and not hear another word about competing.

"This is *not* a requirement," Mr. Conner said.

It wasn't a choice if I wanted to move past Red Oak.

"I've said it before, but I'll remind everyone again that no one has to compete in this or any other show while on the intermediate team," Mr. Conner said. "I've talked with each of you individually, and am happy to do so again at any time, about your plans and goals for this year."

I raised my head so I could see myself in the mirror. My pale skin looked a couple of shades lighter than normal. *Breathe, Lauren,* I told myself. I focused on slowing my heartbeat and looking at Mr. Conner. During my mini freak-out, Mike and Doug had disappeared from the arena.

"In three weeks, Canterwood will be hosting the

season's first schooling show," Mr. Conner said. "Invitations have been extended to nearby academies for their intermediate and advanced riders."

Three. Weeks. Twenty-one days. Five hundred and four hours until showtime.

8

STRANGE AND
RIGHT

"HOME ADVANTAGE!" DREW SAID, PATTING
Polo's neck. The excitement in his voice made me feel a
tiny surge of excitement and competitiveness.

Drew's comment made Mr. Conner smile. "We have
the perks of not traveling and being familiar with our riding spaces," Mr. Conner said. "But don't mistake that as
a leg up. The visiting school's instructors will have taken
that into account in their preparation of riders."

Clare raised her hand and Mr. Conner nodded at her.

"How many classes can we take?" Clare asked.

"Two, maximum," Mr. Conner said. "We can discuss
options, but the choices are ultimately yours. After our
lesson, I'll post a sign-up sheet on the bulletin board near
my office door. If you intend to compete, you have until

midweek to sign up. Next to the sheet, there will be a list of classes available to you. Please write down your choices along with your name."

Mr. Conner motioned to Lexa, who had raised her hand. "How many schools are coming?" she asked.

"RSVPs are still arriving," Mr. Conner said. "I'm guessing three or four academies will attend. When we were deciding to host the show, we made it a priority that this event have every aspect of a schooling show. I made certain to keep the invite list short."

Mr. Conner glanced at our group. His eyes stopped on me for a second before shifting to Lexa. *I wonder if he thinks I won't attend the show,* I thought.

I'd explained to Mr. Conner that I'd come to Canterwood to ease back onto the show circuit. Even though my first reaction to his news had been panic, the feeling had slowly dissipated the more I thought about it. There wouldn't be a more perfect scenario than this to re-enter showing. A smile tugged at the corners of my mouth. This wasn't going to be like before. I wouldn't be riding a different horse or counting points until I racked up enough to become junior champion. At Canterwood, I'd have the first chance to ride my own horse and show for fun. I couldn't wait to show off Whisper!

"If there are no more questions, let's begin today's lesson," Mr. Conner said. "As I'm sure you noticed, Mike and Doug set up a cavaletti course. We'll start with two poles on the ground and increase to four by the end of the lesson. Who can tell me why we might be working with cavaletti?"

Cole raised his hand. "Pacing," he said. "Usually, riders start with a couple of poles on the ground, then raise them and keep adding more, but height isn't the goal. The poles are supposed to help the horse raise his legs higher and pay more attention to the placement of his hooves."

"Exactly," Mr. Conner said. "Great answer, Cole."

Cole smiled, looking down and smoothing a section of Valentino's mane.

"We'll start with two poles on the ground and increase to four by the lesson's end," Mr. Conner said. "I'll add the holders after you've all taken your horses over the ground poles several times."

A giant sneeze came from a few horses away and everyone turned in Clare's direction. Fuego shook his chestnut head, wiggling his upper lip. "Excuse him!" Clare said, giggling. "Giant Kleenex, anyone?"

Everyone laughed. Everyone but Mr. Conner.

Mr. Conner stood, silent, until everyone's attention

was on him again. "Cole brought up what the exercise is supposed to do, but I'd like someone to tell me why it's beneficial for a competition."

I raised my hand.

"Lauren, go ahead," Mr. Conner said.

"Working with cavaletti is important for showing because points can be deducted during equitation and hunter classes because it's dangerous if a horse 'hangs' his hooves. It's also great for jumping in general because it can help prevent accidents."

"Correct," Mr. Conner said. "We won't be able to use the cavaletti to the maximum in one lesson—it will take several practices to have the poles raised in varying heights. I want to work up to trotting over four poles on the ground by the lesson's end."

This session would be good for Whisper and me. The mare's Hanoverian/Thoroughbred blood gave her long strides, but she sometimes rushed jumps, and it threw off our pacing. We'd done some cavaletti work over the summer, but not nearly enough.

Mr. Conner lined us up along the wall in random order. Cole. Riley. Me. Lexa. Drew. Clare.

For the first round, five of us stayed back while Cole took the course twice. Then it was Riley's turn. Both riders had no problems getting Valentino and Adonis to step over the poles.

My turn.

I loosened the reins and tapped my heels against Whisper's sides. She moved forward at a collected walk. We aligned ourselves in front of the cavaletti course. Whisper stepped over the first pole and lifted her hooves higher over the second.

I deepened my seat, turning her around to walk over the cavaletti again. This time Whisper picked up her hooves better over the first pole. She placed each hoof well away from the ground poles.

With a tiny smile, I got back in line and Lexa began the exercise. When each of us completed the *très* basic course, Mr. Conner added a third pole. We started again. Fuego, rushing, took three short strides before the last pole and nicked it with his left back hoof. Clare did a half halt, circled Fuego once, and gave him more space as he walked to the first pole.

"Clare," Mr. Conner called. "Give Fuego a bit more rein and loosen your body so he doesn't feel like you want him to rush."

Clare nodded, her red curls bouncing under her helmet. The liver chestnut, responding to Clare's aids, walked over the cavaletti with ease this time.

With each round, Mr. Conner changed the course. He added a fourth pole, then removed two and raised them a couple of inches off the ground. Soon the third pole was added back in. Whisper, loving the exercise, snapped her knees as she stepped over the low poles. The easy exercise made me happy, too—it bolstered my confidence about jumping.

At the session's end, Mr. Conner brought us in front of him. Whisper half-pranced, tossing her head as we halted. The lesson hadn't winded her, but paying attention to the spacing of the cavaletti had kept her engaged.

"Thank you," Mr. Conner said, addressing us. "I saw improvement with each of you and your horses with each round. Drew, I'm especially impressed with Polo's progress during this exercise."

I glanced over at Drew, who was two horses away, next to Lexa. He smiled and dipped his head at Mr. Conner. "Thank you, sir." He gave Polo's shoulder a hearty pat. I smiled for Drew.

Polo, Drew's blood bay gelding, was an Arab and Thoroughbred mix. You'd never know it by his temperament. The always-calm gelding was an especially strong jumper and, during the beginning of the exercise, it seemed as though he'd eyed the poles as high jumps. Drew had worked through each round to encourage Polo to exert the right amount of energy and not work too hard.

"The exercise you completed is not just for new riders," Mr. Conner said. "Throughout the season, we will be tackling several exercises you may view as 'easy,' but will serve as a good refresher or a way to fine-tune skills."

"I'm glad we're going to practice more of those exercises, Mr. Conner," Riley said. "Adonis and I wouldn't be on the intermediate team this year if you hadn't taught us the importance of keeping up basic skills."

Ugh. Khloe would have fake-vomited if she'd heard that.

"That is the attitude I hope you all adopt," Mr. Conner said. "Tomorrow, we'll step up the degree of difficulty with different exercises. Please plan to stay an extra fifteen minutes. I'll be adding in the new aspect of this year's curriculum—equine care and health."

After I'd cooled Whisper, cleaned her stall, and given her fresh water and hay, I started down the aisle to Mr. Conner's office. I checked my watch—he should have finished with Khloe's advanced class a few minutes ago. I'd purposefully taken my time with Whisper to catch Mr. Conner after his last class.

I paused by the bulletin board on the wall—half corkboard and half whiteboard. I read some of the notes scribbled for students. *Alison Robb—see me after lesson. —Mr. Conner.* The name was unfamiliar. *Must be an older or younger rider.* I shook my head. *Stop stalling, Laur.* I glanced at the paper held with a red tack.

7th Grade Intermediate Team Schooling Show Sign-Up was typed at the top in bold font. Next to that sheet was the promised list of classes. I read down the list, although I already knew what I wanted to do.

I looked back at the sign-up sheet. Names and choices half filled the lined page.

Cole Harris: Cross-country and dressage

Lexa Reed: Dressage and trail riding

Riley Edwards: Horse management and show jumping

Clare Bryant: Pleasure class and show jumping

Drew Adams: Cross-country and pleasure class

My heart pounded in my ears when I picked a pen from the cup on the small wooden table under the board.

Lauren Towers: Dressage and trail riding

I put back the pen, looking back at what I'd just written. I'd just signed up for my *first* show since Red Oak. It seemed strange to see my name on the board with classes next to it. Strange *and* right.

Turning away, I smoothed my shirt and knocked on Mr. Conner's partially open door.

"Come in," he said, looking up from his computer screen. "Hi, Lauren."

"Hello, Mr. Conner. Do you have a minute?"

"Of course. Have a seat." He motioned to the chair in front of his desk and smiled.

I'd been in his office before, but I wasn't used to it. I still expected to walk into Kim's office at Briar Creek. My old instructor's office had photos of past and present riders, including Sasha Silver, decorating the walls. Papers and files had been organized with messy chaos.

Mr. Conner's office was the opposite. Giant black filing cabinets were stacked along the wall behind him, everything on his desktop was in a holder, and a giant monthly calendar spread across his desk had something filled in *every* day.

"Thank you for seeing me," I said. "I wanted to tell you that everyone on my team knows about my accident at Red Oak. It sort of . . . came out this weekend."

"How did your teammates react?" Mr. Conner asked. His voice wasn't stern, like it was during lessons.

"It was a little rocky at first," I admitted. "The more honest I was, the better it went. Everyone's fine now. It feels good that they know. I feel more like part of the team."

Mr. Conner nodded. "That's great, Lauren. I imagine it does feel better to have shared something so heavy with friends and teammates."

"Definitely," I said. "I wanted to tell you because you've been so generous with keeping that to yourself. I really appreciate it, and you needed to know that it's not something you have to hide for me anymore."

"Thank you, Lauren," Mr. Conner said. "No matter how the truth came out, I'm glad you're comfortable with the outcome. I believe it will only bring you and your teammates closer."

"I hope so." We smiled at each other, and Mr. Conner asked if there was anything else I wanted to discuss. It felt as though he were giving me an opportunity to ask about the show.

"I'm all set," I said.

"Great. Come see me anytime," Mr. Conner said.

I left his office and passed the sign-up sheet. I couldn't help but smile.

9

TOTAL SETUP

EVEN THOUGH A STACK OF HOMEWORK waited for me back in my room, I took a detour off the main sidewalk back to Hawthorne. I found an empty bench away from the chatter of campus and nestled under a giant oak tree. The tree was still full and leafy—not giving a hint of fall's approach. I put my bag on the bench and sat, rifling through the GO CCA! green and gold tote until I found my BlackBerry.

I pressed speed dial number three.

"Hey, sis!" Becca answered.

"Hi!" I said. "I'm so happy I caught you. Do you have a sec?"

"Hmmm. Maybe two seconds," Becca said, her tone teasing. "What's up?"

"There's so much. I seriously don't even know where to start. But Saturday morning seems right."

"Oooh. Spill," Becca said.

"It's not really a 'spill' type of thing."

"Uh-oh. I better get comfy for this."

I visualized Becca leaning back into her cozy pillows or sitting in her pod chair, spinning in a slow circle.

"Okay, so you know I had a sleepover last weekend."

"That sounds vaguely familiar. Oh, wait. The bazillion BBMs are bringing it back to me."

"Okay, okay! So there were a *few* messages."

"Your BBM yesterday said it had been great."

"It was," I said quickly. "But—"

"There's a *but*?" Becca cut me off. "Laur, did something happen?"

I drew my feet onto the bench, hugging my knees to my chest. "Mom called on Saturday morning. Everyone had just woken up and we were about to get breakfast in the common room." I walked Becca through the morning, stopping for a breath when I got to the part about seeing myself on TV.

"Oh, my God. Oh, Lauren! You went into the common room and *your* Red Oak trial was playing?!"

I nodded, forgetting she couldn't see me. Phone convos

with Becca always felt like she was next to me. "It was all happening so fast and so slow at the same time. Know what I mean? I just sank down to the floor, not knowing what to do."

"Of course not! Who would? I probably would have run out crying." Becca's tone was mixed with sympathy, anger, and big-sister protectiveness.

"I wanted to run," I said. "But I don't think my legs would have worked."

"You're also not that type of girl," Becca said. "You face stuff like that in the moment."

"I had to. I couldn't do that to Khloe and Lexa or let Riley see the footage and run with it."

Becca listened, letting me talk. It felt beyond good to tell her about yesterday. At home, she was the first one I went to with anything. The best part about Becca? Just because she was my sister didn't mean she wouldn't be honest. If she thought I'd messed up, she'd tell me.

"I just finished my riding lesson and everyone on my team seems cool. I feel so much better that they know. You know how bad I felt about keeping that secret. Especially from Khloe. I wouldn't have felt as though our friendship would have had a real chance to move forward unless I'd been honest with her."

I shifted on the bench, noticing for the first time that the sun was setting. Shadows darkened parts of campus and lightning bugs blinked across the lawn. Time always went by so fast when I talked to my sister.

"I'm glad you feel better and I think you're right about honesty—it's good for your whole team morale. But there's something that just doesn't feel right."

"What?" I asked.

"Laur. Think about it. You said your common room has *hundreds* of DVDs, right?"

"Yeah . . ."

"So, what are the odds that this girl picks *your* horse show out of them? I totally think that Jill chick set you up."

"Jill? No way. She's not like that, Becs. You'd know it if you met her."

"Okay, maybe not Jill. But what about Riley? What if she directed Jill toward your DVD and didn't clue her in? You've told me how ruthless this girl is. All of your friends were gathered, you were out of the room, and she had the *perfect* opportunity."

I played with my necklace. "If I were in your position, I know I'd be saying the same thing to you. But it just doesn't feel like Riley did anything. Everyone *was* there, so Riley wasn't alone to go through the DVDs.

Plus, Jill would have told me if she'd had even an inkling that something was off or if Riley had influenced her in any way."

"You're usually a great judge of character, so I'll take your word on Jill. I still don't know about Riley, though."

"I get it. But Riley also didn't know about Red Oak. Or, at least if she did know, she kept it *very* well hidden."

"Keep an eye on her for the next few days and see how she treats you," Becca said. "Maybe that'll help."

Becca and I spent a few more minutes talking about it, and by the end of our conversation, I remained convinced that the DVD surfacing had been a total coincidence.

"Before we hang up," I said. "What's going on with you and Grant? How's everything at home?"

I heard papers rustling and a familiar click—Becca's desk lamp. There was a *creak*, and I knew she'd sat in her desk chair. It was a chair she'd lugged to our Brooklyn apartment from Tenth Avenue one afternoon when we'd she'd spotted it in someone's FREE! TAKE ME! pile on the sidewalk.

"Grant and I are fabulous," Becs said. I could feel her smile. "He took me to see a romantic comedy last week-end. It was a complete surprise! We'd both agreed on an action flick before we went. At the ticket counter, though, he bought tickets for *Timeless* because he'd heard me talking nonstop about it with my friends."

"Awww! That's so sweet! You're on the hook now to go see some gory boy movie. You know that, right?"

"Of course," Becca said, laughing. "He already picked a zombie flick for next week. But totally worth it. As for home . . . everything's okay at Casa de Towers. I'm busy with school, Mom's working a lot on this big case. She's tried to explain it to me a bunch of times, but she talks in legalese and you know how fluent I am in that." We laughed.

"Lawyer-speak is not a language you and I will ever master," I said.

"So true. Dad's busy with a new book. He's excited about it and in the outline process. He's carrying a notepad everywhere in case he has a new idea."

"Is he bringing notecards to dinner yet?"

"Last night. He tried hiding them under his napkin and Mom caught him." Becca giggled. "Dad looked like a kid who lost his fave toy when Mom took them away from him for dinner."

She told me a few more quick things that were going on at home, and then we hung up.

I stared at my phone, watching the screen dim. Talking

to Becca about home and hearing about Mom and Dad made me feel more and less homesick at the same time. They were still doing all of the same things, but without me. I was missing dinner every night. I didn't get to give Mom advice about what skirt went best with her blazer for a meeting. I wasn't there for Dad as the sun was coming up and he wanted someone to bounce ideas off of. And, maybe the biggest thing of all, I wasn't around Becca.

Remember what you went through to get here, I reminded myself. *Everyone is behind you. No one is moving on without you. They're living, and so are you. Plus, you'll be home soon enough for Thanksgiving break, then Christmas.* I'd get to see my family and Ana, Brielle, and Taylor. To get to break, though, I had to go back to my room and tackle homework. Monday madness, as Khloe and I had dubbed Monday night's homework craze, was way overdue.

10

EYES ON THE PRIZE

HOURS LATER, KHLOE AND I SIMULTANEOUSLY groaned. We were both in pj's and sitting at our desks. It felt like if I sat at mine much longer, I'd mold into my chair.

Khloe's long blond hair was swept up into a messy, beachy bun and a few tendrils that had escaped framed her face. *Très* chic. Her pajamas were so Khloe—a long-sleeve tissue tee with matching drawstring pants. They were both the same hot pink color with purple splotches that looked like an exotic cheetah print.

Mine were a little more subdued. I'd paired flowing ivory pants with an arctic green lacy tank top.

"Monday madness is so wrong," Khloe said. "It's backward! We're coming from two days off—we should be eased back into the school week."

"Totally agree," I said. "Keep our reward in mind."

Khloe rubbed her eyes, smudging her kohl eyeliner. "Manis after we're done. Believe me, I keep repeating that to myself. You promised to teach me an EBT for nails, too."

I smiled. "EBTs" or "essential beauty tricks" were tips that Ana, Brielle, and I had traded. I'd told Khloe about it and she'd adopted the idea, wanting to share EBTs with me.

"I did. Doing our nails will be the perf reward. What do you have left?"

Khloe picked up her hunter green assignment notebook—they were mandatory for all students—and scanned the page. "English and . . . oooh! English and nothing! I got more done than I thought."

"That's major, Khlo! Yay!" I looked at my own notebook. "I've got a history worksheet, then a few math problems need rechecking."

"Nice, LT. I bet we finish at the same time."

"Let's see!" I said, spinning my desk chair back to my work.

Khloe giggled. "You're on."

I filled in blanks and bubbles on the worksheet from Mr. Spellman. I'd just read the text, so I didn't have to hover too long over any answers. It had taken me a little longer than usual, though, because I'd had to read the chapter twice. It was complex and a *lot* was covered in twenty pages. I wouldn't be doing extra assignments to get advanced course credit, though, if I hadn't prepared myself for the class to be tough. I wanted a shining first semester report card with good grades next to challenging courses.

Even though Khloe and I weren't doing anything but homework, I was grateful and happy that I wasn't doing it by myself. If Khloe hadn't been open to my weekend confession, tonight would be *very* different. The vibe in our room couldn't have been more relaxed from our easy chatter to the soft lighting to the vanilla-cupcake-scented Yankee candles that burned on our coffee table.

Focus! I reminded myself. I dove back into my worksheet, determined to finish as fast as possible so we could get to the fun stuff.

"Done, done, done!" Khloe sang. I jumped, almost knocking over my cup of jasmine green tea.

"You scared me!" I said, shaking my head and smiling at the same time. "Somehow I don't think Ms. Utz would have given me extra credit if I'd turned in my paper doused with green tea."

"Sorry!" Khloe said, hiding a smile. She closed her books and started shoving them into her bag. "You close?"

"I . . . am . . ." I kept scribbling ". . . done!"

I hopped up, stepping over to Khloe to high-five her. "Mani time!" I said. "Let me pack up too."

I put each hardback and several workbooks into my book bag. The ones I'd use first in the day went into a small canvas tote with the United States Equestrian Team crest on it. I'd learned to distribute the massive weight of the books between two bags. I zipped up my binder and stuck it inside my backpack.

I finished cleaning off my desktop and putting away my pencils, calculator, and extra notebook, and plopped onto the rug next to Khloe.

"Thanks for grabbing everything," I said. Khloe had pulled out our plastic bin of nail polish we'd stored together, cotton balls, polish remover, and each of our nail kits.

"No prob. I have *no* idea what color I want," Khloe said.

"Me either."

We looked into the plastic tub, staring inside at the rainbow variety of colors. I pushed aside a couple of bottles and saw iridescent OPI lavender.

"Do you like this?" I asked Khloe, holding up the bottle.

"Love," she said. "It'll be pretty with your hair and eyes. Smart to go light, too, because no one will see the chips."

"Very true. Then this is it." I smiled. "What about you?"

"I think . . ." Khloe picked up a shimmery teal shade from Essie. "Does this look mermaidlike?"

"Definitely very Ariel. That's such a fun shade."

"Yay! That's just what I wanted. I love our colors."

We unzipped each of our nail kits and got to work on maintenance. I swiped polish remover over my nails to remove any traces of possibly-still-lingering polish, then squeezed cuticle oil onto my nails and rubbed it in. The oil's scent made me relax, and when I blinked, I realized how heavy my eyelids were.

You're not ninety! It's only 9:45. I rolled my eyes at myself.

"How was your lesson?" Khloe asked. She had an orange stick in one hand.

"Great. Mr. Conner took us back to the basics with cavaletti. Whisper really had to think about where she was stepping."

"That's smart. Mr. Conner did something similar with

my class last week. He had us do games on horseback. It reminded me of gymkhanas at summer riding camp."

"Oh, fun! Wow, that makes me think of egg and spoon races, costume classes, relays . . ." I smiled. "We should have a game day just because!"

"We *so* should. I would love to take on a certain someone in a relay." Khloe cleared her throat. "Speaking of *someone*, how is Riley during lessons?"

"She hasn't been outright mean, but she's always *there*. If she's not talking to Clare, she's around me whenever I don't want her to be."

"Like when?" Khloe filed her thumbnail.

"Like today, when I was talking to Drew."

I put up a hand as Khloe's eyebrows went up. "Talking!" I said. "That's it. I was talking to him, and during those thirty seconds, Riley realized she needed to ask Drew about an assignment."

"Sounds like someone's jealous."

"I know she likes Drew. But is she that insecure that I can't even *talk* to him without her jumping in?"

"Yes." Khloe shook her head. "She's probably especially insecure around you."

I looked up from my pinky, which I'd been filing. "What do you mean?"

"Well, you're the most experienced rider on the team. Clearly. That's something Riley can't deny. You're also comfortable around guys. You're not afraid to talk to them, and I've seen how they respond to you."

"Whoa, you're making me sound like some kind of guy expert," I said. "I am cool around most guys, but *you're* the one who got asked out." I grinned, then stuck out my tongue.

"Touché," Khloe said. "I really just meant that your background in riding is spreading around the stable, and you already were popular before people knew about that. You're also making more nonrider friends each day you're here. Riley won't give up her seat on the throne as seventh grade queen bee easily."

I picked up the bottle of base coat. "She can have it. I'm not chasing popularity, and I don't want people to befriend me just because of old titles. I mean, I've already got *the* Khloe Kinsella as my bestie; what more does a girl need?"

Khloe grinned. "That's true."

We went back to our nails, and I replayed the conversation in my head. It felt *off*. It almost seemed like Khloe thought I'd ditch her or that I'd have every guy in our grade looking at me. Like Zack, maybe. Or even Drew.

Drew's face popped into my brain. I hadn't thought about our boy conversation until now, but when Khloe had described her dream guy, Drew Adams was a ten. *But Khloe likes Zack, obviously,* I argued with myself. She wasn't faking excitement over her run-in with him this afternoon.

"Oooh, I almost forgot," Khloe said. "Did Mr. Conner talk to your class about the schooling show?"

I looked up from my hand. The clear base polish on my pointer finger was gloopy, as if I'd painted it five times. Oops.

"He did," I said, quickly painting my other nails and handing the bottle to Khloe. "Our sign-up sheet was the only one on the board. Did he talk to your team?"

Khloe nodded. "We start signing up tomorrow. I'm so excited!" She put down the base coat bottle and waved her hand with wet nails in the air. "How are you feeling about it?"

"Scared at first. I kind of froze and couldn't even think. But when I calmed down, I was happy about getting to show with Whisper for the first time. It was even hard to pick only two classes. I like how this show isn't so serious and that there are some fun classes."

"I'm so happy you're showing!" Khloe said, putting

down her hand. "That's huge. What classes did you pick?"

"Dressage and trail riding," I said. "I couldn't pass up the trail riding class."

"I chose those, too! You're so right about trail riding—it doesn't feel like a class. I can't wait." Khloe smiled. "I'm really, *really* happy you're showing, LT. It's going to be your comeback."

"We'll see about that, but thanks! I can't wait to see you and Ever compete."

"It's going to be the best weekend," Khloe said. She looked at her nails. "Okay, pause for a sec. I'm ready for polish. Got an EBT for me?"

"I do! So, first, don't shake the polish bottle. Roll it between your palms like this." I rolled mine and Khloe mimicked my movements. "Shaking the bottle creates bubbles and those can mess up your polish."

"I never thought about that," Khloe said. "Good tip."

"One more. When you paint your nails, finish your first coat by swiping the brush horizontally across the bottom of your nails. It makes them harder to chip."

"Cool! I'm going to have the best nails ever. Now I've got to think of EBTs for you."

Smiling, Khloe and I applied our polishes. We laughed

and talked more and more as lights-out approached. I pushed the weird conversation out of my head, content that I'd overthought Khloe's comments. When we snuggled into our beds hours later, our lavender and teal nails were *très magnifique.*

II

SHE HAS A . . . DATE?

"LT!"

I stopped midstep on my way to the math building and turned toward the voice. Cole Harris waved and hurried up the sidewalk to catch up to me. His leather messenger bag was slung across his chest and he wore an espresso-colored polo shirt that brought out his green eyes.

"Hey!" I said. "Where have you been hiding?"

Cole shook his head. "Under a stack of books at the library. Of course, they're all research books that I can't check out. Like anyone else is going to need biographies about Sue Monk Kidd at the *exact* time I do."

"I don't know," I teased. "Her fan club might want access to those twenty-four seven."

We laughed. The September sun had burned off the early morning fog and we'd moved just off the sidewalk as students hurried to their first classes. Usually, Khloe and I left Hawthorne together, but she'd stayed behind. She'd misplaced a science paper and had told me to go without her so I wouldn't be late.

"What class do you have?" Cole asked.

"Math. You?"

"Gym. *First* period."

Cole and I made similar grumbling sounds.

"Sorry," I said, wrinkling my nose. "No one wants gym first period."

"Especially when Mr. Warren makes us do chin-ups," Cole said. "I'd rather play dodgeball and toss a projectile, thank you."

"Same. I'll keep my fingers crossed for you."

The math and gymnasium were in the same direction, so we kept walking together.

"I'm glad we ran into each other," Cole said. "We haven't gotten a chance to talk. Mr. Conner doesn't make it easy to chat during lessons."

I shifted my bag from one hand to the other. "We *can* chat during riding. Then we'd have *plenty* of time to talk while we're on stall-mucking duty together."

Cole laughed. "I like dishing with you, but not enough to muck stalls."

"I do want to talk about what Lexa told you," I said. "Any chance you want to grab something at The Sweet Shoppe after our lesson?"

We stopped near the entrance to the math building.

"Sounds perf," Cole said. "Meet you out front after riding?"

I nodded. "Done. See you in fashion class."

Cole smiled and we separated.

I hurried up the stairs and pulled open the glass door to the building. I walked down the hallway, doing a quick check of my outfit. I'd paired a black A-line skirt with camel-colored knee-high socks and nude peep-toe booties with a low wedge. Khloe had loaned me a royal blue shirt with capped sleeves and a crew neckline. I'd curled my hair with a big barreled curling iron this morning.

I walked into Ms. Utz's classroom and, spotting Lexa, snagged the desk next to her.

"Hey and *wow*," Lexa said. "You look so great."

"*Excusez-moi?* Are you saying I've looked awful every other day?" I put down my bag and crossed my arms, pretending to be offended.

"Yes. That's *exactly* what I said," Lexa teased. "Your

outfits are always great, but it looks like you did something extra this morning. What's up?"

"Nothing. I *am* wearing Khloe's shirt. Maybe you remember seeing it on her?"

Lexa scanned me. "Hmm. I remain unconvinced."

Citrusy body spray wafted through the air. Glancing up, I sneezed and Riley stared in my direction as she headed toward the last row of desks near the window.

"So glad she's sitting far away," I whispered to Lexa. "She looked at me like I'm infected with the plague."

"Plague brought on by her body-spray bath." Lexa giggled. "And, seriously, are you sure there's nothing going on that you want to talk about?"

"Nope, I promise. I just felt like dressing up a little and putting more effort into my hair."

"This has nothing to do with . . . oh . . . I don't know, a certain guy?"

I felt a flush spread from my neck to my cheeks. "Drew?"

Lexa tilted her head. "Unless there are more boys that I haven't seen you with . . ."

"I did *not* dress up for Drew! We were just talking yesterday—"

"*And* before our riding lesson. He's so crushing on you!" Lexa grinned, pulling out her textbook.

"He is not! I'd know if he was. Drew's a really nice guy and I like talking to him."

"I saw," Lex said. "And so did Riley."

"Riley saw us *talking*. There's nothing I can do if she's jealous over that." I reached into my own bag, pulling out my orange-and-white textbook, notebook, pencil, and calculator.

"It's like boy fever is everywhere! First Khloe and Zack. Now you and Drew. I can't imagine what it was like in your room last night. Khloe must have *freaked* about Friday. She's been BBMing me nonstop—sometimes just a row of exclamation points."

I shifted to face Lexa head-on. "What's Friday?"

She frowned. "Khloe didn't tell you? Zack texted her last night and asked her out. She told him yes, and she's been freaking out ever since."

I shook my head, confused. "Are you sure? We did our nails and homework together last night. She didn't say anything about a date with Zack. I knew he'd asked her out, but not with a set date and everything."

My mind went through every second of last night. Khloe's phone had buzzed once, but she hadn't looked at it. She'd silenced it. After our nails, we'd washed our faces and read. I turned out my light first. Zack must have texted *after*

I'd fallen asleep. This morning had been frenzied, but not much more so than a regular day. A definite date with Zack seemed like something Khloe would want to tell me ASAP.

Lexa stared at her desktop. "Laur, I *know* Khloe wanted to tell you. She texted me really late last night and said you were already asleep. I'm sure she was two seconds away from shaking you awake."

I wanted to believe Lexa, but hearing about Zack this way stung. Khloe had had every opportunity to tell me this morning. This was exactly what I'd been afraid would happen after Saturday—Khloe was mad but not saying so. Somebody bumped my desk with a book bag and I didn't even look up.

"She didn't say anything about it this morning, though. Lex, has she said anything to you about being mad about Red Oak? If she has, please tell me. I promise I won't say a word to Khloe that you told me."

Lexa sighed and rested her chin on her hand. "She hasn't said anything about it, Lauren. Not a word. I know Khloe, and if she was upset, she'd go to you. She's not the passive-aggressive type."

"I'm sorry to have asked you," I said. "I didn't mean to put you in a weird spot. I'll talk to Khloe."

"Good," Lexa said. "I'm sure there's a silly explanation

and you'll be a thousand percent okay after you talk to her."

I smiled at Lexa. I was glad, though, when Ms. Utz walked into the room. The distraction was welcome. I'd pay attention, not obsess over the Khloe and Zack thing, then I'd go to English and talk to Khloe.

"Good morning, class," Ms. Utz said. She towered over the classroom even though she wore flats. Her hair was up in its usual tight bun. "Please pass last night's homework forward. When I've collected that, I'll hand back your homework from yesterday."

We turned in our homework, and Ms. Utz moved to the front of the room, holding a stack of papers in her hands. "It seems as though some of you might not have a grasp of the material," she said. "If this is true, please come talk to me during office hours. Several of these papers were disappointing, especially those with careless mistakes."

Ms. Utz began placing our papers facedown on our desks. Lexa got hers and grimaced. She flipped up the corner so I could see. C+.

"It's just homework," I whispered when Ms. Utz moved near Riley's end of the room. "Tiny percentage of our grade."

Lexa nodded. She put the paper into a folder and stuffed it into her bag.

Ms. Utz reached me, putting my paper on the desk. I peeked at it. A-. I let out a breath. Lexa's grade and Ms. Utz's speech had made me nervous! I put my paper in the left side of my file for completed homework.

Lexa made a tiny noise and I glanced over. *What'd you get?* she mouthed.

I didn't want to make her feel bad, but I didn't want to lie. "A minus," I whispered. "Sorry."

Lexa shook her head. "Good job," she whispered back.

"Everyone should have his or her paper now," Ms. Utz said.

A few whispers were scattered across the room. Ms. Utz stood, arms folded, at the front of the room. It was as if no one noticed, though, because the hushed chatter didn't stop.

"Clearly, some of you are already bored," Ms. Utz said. "My speaking isn't holding your attention, so you all will do the talking."

The whispering stopped. Students shot each other *it's your fault!* looks. Lexa and I made *ugh* faces when Ms. Utz wasn't looking.

"I'll call a random name, and that person will step up

to the board. I'll give you a problem similar to last night's homework and you'll solve it, showing all of your work and talking the rest of the class through your decision step by step."

Ms. Utz walked from the front of the room and sat behind her desk, turning her chair so she could see us and the whiteboard.

"We'll solve problems until the bell. Your homework for tonight will be the next lesson and the thirty problems that follow," Ms. Utz said. Sunlight shifted outside and faded out of the room, making the fluorescent lights feel harsh.

A girl, Amanda, raised her hand. Multicolored bangles clinked down her arm. "Ms. Utz? If we're doing problems until the bell, how are we going to learn the lesson to complete tonight's homework?"

Ms. Utz smiled, showing her square teeth. "After class, whenever you have free time, you're going to use the new online lectures for my class. This is the *perfect* time to see how well you learn via prerecorded lessons."

I tapped my eraser against my notebook. Either Ms. Utz was still *really* mad from our talking or she was just in a bad mood today. I'd never tried a lecture via the computer. What if I had a question and didn't understand some of the material? I couldn't exactly ask my laptop.

"The lessons are forty minutes long and they cover sample problems, just like in class lessons," Ms. Utz said. "If you have questions, please e-mail me."

Forty minutes?! I wanted to smack my head with my textbook. That added almost an extra hour of homework tonight.

"Brice," Ms. Utz called. "Please come up to the board."

While Ms. Utz called names, I went through the calendar in my homework planner and added the lecture. Today's space was already a quarter full.

And this was only my first class.

12

FYI: INTENSE BLUE EYES SCRAMBLE YOUR BRAIN.

AFTER MATH, I LEFT THE BUILDING AND soaked up the sunlight hitting my shoulders. I'd been called on twice in class. One problem I'd gotten right and I'd stumbled on the second, finally reaching an answer that didn't match when I checked my work. Ms. Utz had me back up, go through the problem over again, and retrace my steps until I found my mistake. I'd looked at the class and caught Riley stifling a yawn.

I was *not* going to let one long class drag me down. I headed for the history building, happy that I'd see Khloe in class.

"Lauren, hey."

A strong, smooth voice jolted me out of my thoughts. Drew walked up one of the many off-the-main-path sidewalks. He looked undeniably cute in a red T-shirt, dark wash jeans, and black Converse.

"Hi! What's up?" My words came out all bubbly and high-pitched. My cheeks warmed.

"Heading to science. You?" Drew stepped closer, stopping only a couple of feet away.

"History. Just got out of the longest math class ever." I smiled. I felt more like myself with every passing second.

"Sorry," Drew said. "Math's not my favorite. At least we have gym today and that's a free pass."

He remembered that we *have gym together today.* My thoughts seemed to scramble in my brain. Drew's intense blue eyes met mine and *that* definitely didn't help!

"Yeah. Right. Gym. Easy." So, one-word sentences were all I could muster. If Brielle and Ana were here, they'd be staring at me and thinking, *Where's our LT?*

Drew grinned. "Hopefully, Coach Warren will let us do whatever."

"What would you do?" I asked.

"Hit the track. I love running. I'm not on the track team or anything, but it clears my head. It's a different kind of workout than swimming. I'm in total competition mode when I swim."

"I run too." I smiled, shifting my bag. "I know what

you mean about it clearing your head. Whatever problems I'm dealing with disappear when I run."

"If we get a free period for gym, maybe come find me on the track?"

I nodded. "But it'll be the other way around. I'll be the girl overlapping you."

He laughed, then made a mock-serious face. "A challenge, huh? I'll be ready. See you in gym, Towers."

Trading smiles, we split up. Maybe I had to ease up with this zero-boy policy. Yes, I'd been at Canterwood for almost a week and a half. Yes, I'd vowed to focus on riding and school for a while. I also didn't want to miss anything. If there was potential for Drew and me to become closer friends and possibly more, I owed it to myself to at least be open-minded.

This was a time when I needed my besties from home! I pulled out my BlackBerry and opened our group chat.

Lauren:

Know u guys r in class, but I have boy news 2 tell u! Any1 4 Skype 2nite?

I felt better after sending the message. Brielle and Ana would know what to do.

"Hey!" Zack called, waving at me from yards away. Garret, his friend, was beside him. He waved, too.

"Hi!" I called back.

The need to talk to Khloe about Zack resurfaced full force. I'd managed to keep it in check until now. Khloe had been so excited about his response to her silly text pic—she'd told me right away. Despite what Lexa had said, I still couldn't understand why Khloe hadn't told me about her date. She'd had plenty of time to BBM. Even just a *Got big news to share!!* would have made everything okay.

I pulled open the heavy wooden door to the history building. All of my focus was on finding Khloe. I didn't even slow to take in the beauty of the building, the way I had every day since I'd arrived. I hurried past the stained-glass windows, under the arched beams of the ceiling, and past the quotes of famous historical figures painted on the walls.

When I reached Mr. Spellman's classroom, I looked for blond hair. Khloe, sitting in the middle of the classroom, saw me and smiled. My stomach felt like I'd eaten too much Halloween candy.

I settled into a seat in the row next to Khloe and put down my bag.

"Hey, hey," Khloe said. "How's your day? I haven't had a second to BBM or anything! Crazy!"

So, she wasn't going to say anything right away. Warning bells chimed in my head.

"Good," I said. "I ran into Lexa this morning. We chatted for a bit." I stopped, wanting her to jump in.

"Cool. I'm glad you saw Lex! I'm sorry I couldn't leave with you this morning. Ugh. It was one of those mornings where I lose everything possible."

I leaned down, pulling out my thick history textbook, homework folder, and assignment notebook.

"Khlo, I don't want to let things get weird, so I want to just say it. When I saw Lexa, she told me something about you and Zack."

Khloe's brown eyes, lids dusted with a shimmery mink color, widened. "Oh, no. Oh, Laur. She told you that Zack asked me out last night."

I nodded.

"Lauren, I am *so* sorry. I know how awful this looks. If I were you, I'd be mad and hurt. Please let me explain. I got the text after you'd fallen asleep. I almost had to tie myself down to stop from waking you up!" She shook her head. "I was such a bad roommate. I started making noise in my closet hoping it would wake you."

"You could have for *that* news," I said. "That's huge."

"I wanted to! You were in such a deep sleep and I knew

how exhausted you were from the past few days. On a whim, I texted Lexa to see if she was awake. She's usually in bed fairly early. But she was up and I told her about Zack."

I nodded again. My head was going to bobble off if I kept this up.

Khloe chewed her bottom lip. She looked as sad as I felt.

"Everything was a mess this morning. I was *dying* to tell you—seriously dying—but I wanted to talk about it when we had time. There is so much to talk about—not just 'OMG, Zack asked me out!' but what did that mean, how much did he *really* like me, what prep were we going to do for Friday. You know? I wanted it to be an after-school, in-our-pj's convo with snacks. Not when we were rushing out the door to class."

Everything Khloe said made sense. I *had* been tired, and of course she'd wanted to make it into a big moment—that was Khloe. And Zack officially asking her out was huge.

"Lexa caught me off guard," I said. "My feelings were hurt because you'd told her and hadn't said a word about it to me all morning."

Khloe hung her head, her shoulders drooping.

"*But* Lexa wouldn't have said anything if she didn't think you'd already told me. She wasn't trying to rub it in that she knew first. If it were me and I had news like that, I'd probably think the same thing as you. I'd want the right moment to talk about it."

Khloe lifted her head a little, meeting my eyes.

"I understand where you're coming from," I said. "I'm not mad. I get it. *And* I'm crazy excited!"

"OhthankyouLauren!" Khloe's words ran together. She reached across the aisle, arms outstretched, and we hugged. I smelled Khloe's familiar Coach Poppy perfume and coconut-scented shampoo. I couldn't be mad at her. She'd been trying to do the right thing and I could *feel* how genuinely sorry she was.

"'Course, Khlo. I want to hear *everything* and when we find the right time—"

"Um, we're going to *make* the right time!" Khloe interrupted, grinning. "Tonight, after riding, want to get into cozies and talk before homework?"

"Hmm . . ." I pretended to think about it. "Yes! I want to hear the complete play-by-play—what you thought when you saw his text, how long you took to write back, what you said word for word. All of it."

Khloe silently clapped her hands. "Yay!"

The classroom door closed with a thud. I looked up, not even noticing the room had filled with students.

I looked over at Khloe. "We okay?" she asked.

"Very okay."

Mr. Spellman was bent over his desk. He ran a hand through his dark hair peppered with gray. I noticed another odd figurine had been added to his desk—an owl with wide yellow eyes. Very Mr. Spellman. He'd quickly become one of my fave teachers. His advanced class wasn't easy, but I liked history.

"Morning, everyone," he said.

"Good morning," we said.

"Let me run through attendance, then I'll pass back the classwork you completed yesterday."

He called down the roll and I got out the rest of my supplies, waiting until he called "Lauren Towers" before responding with a wave of my hand.

He gathered our stack of papers and began handing them out. During yesterday's class he'd given each of us a lined paper with a question to answer. Each of us had received a different question that corresponded to the reading we'd done the night before. The prompts had to be in short essay format.

There was an optional extra credit question at the

bottom that we were allowed to try once we'd answered the main question. Luckily, I'd had enough time last night to answer the main prompt and extra credit question. The topics had covered the early American colonies—something I was familiar with—so I felt fairly confident that my grade would be good.

Mr. Spellman stopped beside me, placing my paper on my desktop. I turned it over and put it flat on my desk.

In the upper right corner a small D+ had been circled. Comments swam in front of me, but I couldn't even read them.

D+. It didn't register. D+. *Oh, mon Dieu! D+?!* I flipped the paper over, slowly, not wanting to draw attention to myself. I fought the burn that threatened to turn my ears, face, and neck red.

Khloe looked at me. *Okay?* she mouthed.

"Fine," I whispered.

Mr. Spellman reached Khloe and I saw the B+ on her paper. Khloe was uninterested in her paper, though; she went back to watching me. I could feel her question coming, but I pretended to be looking for something in my assignment notebook. Mr. Spellman finished passing out the papers and there wasn't time for her to push me more about my grade.

It was beyond mortifying and too embarrassing to tell

anyone! I'd read and reread the chapter before I'd come to class. Plus, I had come into the class *knowing* about the British colonies. The second I got out of history and could lock myself in the privacy of the girls' bathroom, I was going over my paper. I had no idea where I'd gone wrong.

For the remainder of the period, I was a model student. Not one BBM to anyone. Notes on everything Mr. Spellman said. Volunteering to read aloud passages from our book. Copying due dates from the board. But none of those things made me feel better.

The bell rang and Khloe reached for my arm. "You okay? You were like superstudent Lauren."

"I'm okay," I said. "I didn't get the best grade on my paper and I was doing my overcompensating act." I looked down at my notebook. "I think I took six pages of notes. Need any?"

Khloe smiled. "Maybe later. Hey, sorry about your grade. You work really hard and it was just one assignment. I know you'll pull it up."

"Thanks." I didn't want to talk about it anymore. In fact, I didn't want to look at it either. "Ready to leave for English?"

Khloe and I gathered our things and left. I wished I could leave my grade behind too.

13

SUGAR HEAVEN

I INHALED THE TANTALIZING FALL SMELLS OF apple cider and pumpkin pie that made The Sweet Shoppe smell like heaven. I slid into an empty booth to wait for Cole. The cushy blue booth with a white rectangular table in front of me was adorable. Everything about this place helped me forget about my awful history grade. A cup of tea would soothe the last of my rattled nerves.

Cole walked in, not a minute late, and spotted me. "Hi, Laur," he said, sliding across from me. He put his messenger bag next to him.

"Hey," I said. "I'm *so* excited about the cooler weather menu."

Cole waved his hand. "You haven't seen anything yet.

They somehow manage to keep concocting fresh menu items every season. Soon they'll start adding Halloween and then Christmas-themed stuff."

"Too cool! It's like a quainter, nicer Starbucks with more options."

Cole nodded. "Definitely. I'm glad you wanted to meet up. Want something to eat and drink? My treat."

"You don't have to—"

Cole waved me off. "What'll it be? Some kind of tea and . . ."

Major hearts that he remembered my tea love! "Cinnamon apple tea and a dessert of your choice to split if you want would be perfect. Thank you."

Cole smiled. "Be right back."

Cole was the sweetest. I wanted to hang out with him more—he seemed like such a nice guy. He got in line behind a couple of students. He wasn't hard to spot in breeches and paddock boots among the students in regular clothes. I pulled out my BlackBerry and saw messages.

Brielle:

Can't talk 2nite. Tmrw?

Ana:

Free 2nite!

I typed back to both.

Lauren:

B, no worries! Tmrw 4 sure. Ana, yay! C u in a bit.

I couldn't talk long because of my load of homework, but I needed to see someone from home. Khloe was studying with Clare, so I could talk freely to Ana about my roomie worries.

Cole came back, carrying two lidded orange cups in a cardboard holder. A plate of sugar cookies was in his other hand.

"This is awesome. Thanks, Cole!"

"No prob. Next dessert's on you." He sat, smiling.

"What'd you get?" I asked.

"Pumpkin spice latte," he said. "I drink so much of these every year that I get sick of them by the season's end. I swear I'll never drink another. But that feeling disappears *every* year."

We laughed.

"So," I said. "I want to thank you, first, for not being angry with me because of my secret. Lexa told me how cool you were when she told you. I appreciate your understanding more than I can tell you."

Cole wrapped his hands around his drink, nodding. "Laur, of course. You haven't even been here a *month*. I'm sure it made you feel awful enough to keep that kind of thing to yourself, so what good would it do for any of us to be mad? We're teammates, but I'd like to be friends."

"Me too," I said.

"I know Lexa told you about my past experiences with bullies. When I first got to Canterwood, I felt as though I had to keep it a secret that I was a rider who loved fashion or I'd get beaten up."

My chest burned as if I'd scalded it with tea. "It's so cruel what happened to you. I'm sorry."

"They were ignorant," Cole said. "I think they were afraid to breathe the same air."

I clenched my teeth.

"This isn't about me. I just wanted you to know that I *understand*. You can talk to me any time if you want."

What I wanted to do was to hug him. "Thank you so much. Same for you. Here . . ."

I pulled out my phone. "What's your number?"

Cole told me and I typed it in. I sent him a BBM and heard a jingle in his bag. "Now you have my number too," I said. "Text me or call whenever."

We raised our drinks and touched them together in a toast.

"How're you doing with classes and everything?" Cole asked, biting into a sugar cookie.

My D+ flashed in front of my eyes. I'd kept the paper hidden at the bottom of my bag all day. I hadn't been able to bring myself to read the comments.

"I thought I was doing okay," I said. "But I got a D+ on history homework today. It shook my confidence a little. Well, a lot."

"If it helps, I got an F on my first English assignment at Canterwood," Cole said. "It was homework, too. I managed to get my grade back up and finish with an A-."

"That does help. It really scared me. I haven't told anyone, either. I usually tell Khloe everything, but I feel like she was kind of expecting this to happen."

Cole scrunched his nose. "What you mean? That doesn't seem like Khloe."

"Not like she thought I was a bad student," I said quickly. "More like she and Lex have been saying I'm taking too many advanced classes. I didn't want to tell them about the grade and prove their point. Like you said, it's homework, and I can pull it up."

"I'm sure you can do it," Cole said, pushing the cookie plate toward me. "I know Lex very well, and she wouldn't say any of that if it wasn't coming from a good place."

"It totally was," I said. "I've been keeping long study

hours, but it's just until I get used to the workload here."

"As long as you're not overwhelmed, then go for it. It's definitely not hurting your riding!"

I grinned. "Today was all Whisper. You and Valentino weren't exactly slackers, either."

Cole smiled, taking a sip of coffee. Mr. Conner had upped the difficulty of today's lesson and had worked our class through several exercises that had left my arms and legs burning. He'd verbally quizzed us at the end on material we were supposed to have read the night before in our horse owner's handbook. Luckily, the one question I didn't know had gone to Drew, who'd known the answer.

"What did you just think of . . . ?" Cole asked, pulling me out of my memory. "You just got the biggest grin on your face."

"No!" I said. "I . . . was just . . ."

"Ohhh, look out. You're turning pink. That's the color your skin turns when you're not thinking about *anything*?"

I tossed a wadded-up straw wrapper at him. "Oh, geez. Okay, okay!" I laughed. "I thought about our lesson and then . . ."

Cole's light brown eyebrows raised. "And then . . . ?"

"I thought about Drew. I think he likes me. Or, I think I like him. I don't know!"

Cole put both palms on the table. "You and Drew? You guys would be the cutest couple! LT! You like him—you know you do."

"It's so complicated! I just got out of a relationship before I came here. I promised myself I'd focus on riding and school. Plus, I just got that history grade. That's not exactly a sign to spend time seeing if there's anything between Drew and me."

"One thing at a time. Are you over the first guy?"

Taylor's face popped into my head. "Yes," I said. "I still like him as a friend, though."

"Sounds like it couldn't have been a better breakup. Now, yes, you got a bad grade and you want to focus on academics and riding. *But* you can't stop your feelings. If you don't let yourself explore this thing with Drew, are you going to be able to shut him out completely? Or will you spend as much time *thinking* about him as if you actually felt things out?"

Cole's question made me pause. Really pause. Cole ate another cookie while everything he said spun around in my brain.

"As much as I tell myself to focus on stuff other than Drew, I can't," I said. "I keep wondering if he likes me like I think he does, seeing if he's into anyone else. I think you're right—I can give this maybe-we-like-each-other thing a try. It doesn't mean my grades will sink or that it'll hurt my riding."

"Something you're not saying is that giving Drew a shot might actually make you happy," Cole said. He tilted his head. "That's important, too. Grades and riding are up there—I get it. But so is having fun. Drew is a good person. We're not best friends, but he's always been nice to me and I've never seen him act like a jerk."

I rolled my shoulders. "I just don't want to fail here. At anything."

"You're *so* aware of that," Cole said. "Unless you stop turning in work and start skipping riding lessons, I really think you're going to be fine. Plus, Drew has classes just like you. And he's a rider. *And* he's cute. Pretty perfect, I think."

I smiled. "I had gym with him today. Coach Warren let us do whatever we wanted outside. Drew and I met on the track and ran laps during the period."

Cole smiled, a dimple showing in his right cheek. "And?"

"It was fun. He's competitive, like I am. We pushed each other and were so out of breath we were barely able to talk. He asked me a lot of questions."

"I've seen you around him at lessons," Cole said. "You're a smart girl. You already know that he likes you."

I drained my tea. "Please! I barely know him. How do I know Drew's not like that with everyone?"

Cole shook his head, rolling his eyes in what I knew was pretend annoyance, and gathered our trash. "BBM me when he asks you out."

14

FORGIVE AND FORGET

LUNCH PERIOD CAME FAST TODAY, I THOUGHT, heading into the caf. Today had been going so much better than yesterday. I'd been on my game from the second I'd woken up. First period until now had been smooth, and I wondered if my talks with Cole *and* Ana had something to do with it.

Last night, I'd Skyped with Ana for half an hour. Almost the entire time I'd known her, Ana had been anti-boyfriend. An artist, she wanted to concentrate on drawing and riding. She didn't want to spend time on guys. Brielle and I had been different. We'd both been boy crazy, and we could talk about cute guys for hours. Ana would sketch on whatever scrap of paper was in reach when Bri and I started dishing about guys.

The Ana I'd talked to last night, though, was the same artsy Ana but with a *boyfriend*. She and Jeremy, a *très* cute boy at Yates, had been dating since the end-of-school dance. Ana updated me about her relationship status (awesome!), school (too much homework), Brielle (busy), and art (trying oil painting). She'd been very, no, *extremely* encouraging of the idea of Drew. Pre-Jeremy Ana would have given me the opposite advice. Ana had been so upbeat about Drew that I hadn't wanted to stop talking about him. I'd pushed my Khloe worries aside and hadn't said a word.

I'd been packing my book bag last night when Khloe had come in from Clare's. During the hours of homework, I'd thought about the Khloe and Zack date thing. Khloe wasn't the type of girl to keep anything to herself. If she was mad at me because I hadn't told her about Red Oak sooner, she'd tell me. For the hundredth time, I reached the *same* conclusion. I was tired and overthinking things. When Khloe had gotten settled, I'd plopped next to her in front of the TV and asked if I could tell her about my chat with Cole. The talk had immediately turned to Drew, and Khloe had squealed so loudly that I waited for Christina to come in and point out that it was way past lights-out.

This morning, Khloe had a perma-grin on her face

whenever I said the D-word and had been BBMing me every class to see if I'd run into him in the hallway. She'd also given my outfit the Khloe Kinsella SOA (seal of approval.) I'd paired dark brown knee-high boots with skinny jeans and a button-down peach-colored shirt. Silver hoops, wavy hair, and a spritz of Vera Wang's Princess perfume, something I saved for special occasions, and I was set.

"KK!" I called, seeing Khloe start into the caf. Her shiny blond hair was in a low ponytail secured with a hot pink elastic. She'd paired an electric blue T-shirt with boot-cut whiskered jeans and a pair of my ballet flats. Definite SOA.

"Hey," Khloe said, linking her free arm through mine. "I'm starving!"

"Me too. I'm getting two sandwiches, I swear!"

"So, you haven't seen him at all?" Khloe's voice was a stage whisper.

"No!" I whispered back. "But maybe I'll see him during lunch. If not, riding for sure."

Khloe pouted. "You have to see him before riding. This outfit is so *amaze*. You look cute in breeches, too, but I want Drew to see you in this outfit. Like, now!"

I laughed. "I kind of do too. And what about you? How much Zack spotting since last time we BBMed?"

Khloe paused, her hand hovering above the soda selections. "Zero." She grabbed a Dr Pepper. "So. Tragic."

I hid a smile. "Very tragic, K. I'm sorry you haven't
seen him. But we need girl time to get you ready for your
date. When we sit down, we'll start a list from hair masks
to predate facials and makeup."

Khloe brightened. "Really? Omigod, I would love that."

We filled our trays with honey-roasted turkey sandwiches on wheat bread, scoops of macaroni, and slices of
apple pie. I went back and grabbed a bottle of water, then
we swiped our meal cards.

We stepped into the sunny caf. Tables of various
shapes fit the ginormous room like a jigsaw puzzle. Clare
and Riley were in the middle with two girls that I sort
of recognized from Hawthorne. Another girl walked over
and sat down. Riley, in a capped-sleeve red dress with a
skinny black belt, was the clear leader. I glanced at Khloe,
seeing she'd noticed too.

"Is Riley building an army?" I joked.

"Wouldn't doubt it." Khloe's tone was flat. "At the
very least she's building a collection of friends. Destina-
tion: the top of the popularity chain. I'm using the word
'friends' loosely."

"Gross."

We weaved around the other tables and I kept my chin up, trying not to make it obvious that I was looking for Drew. He wasn't with the guys sitting along the far wall. I didn't see him at the tables under the windows. The swim team—nope. He—

"Laaauuren," Khloe said, grinning. "I highly recommend you scout the room for Drew once you've put down your lunch tray. Otherwise, you're going to end up with macaroni stains down your shirt."

I jerked my gaze away from the windows. "I was just checking!" I said, my voice octaves higher than normal. Ugh! I hated this! This was *so* not me. I didn't get tongue-tied or flustered around guys. The last thing I wanted was to turn into one of those guy-obsessed giggly girls who twirled their hair and thought acting dumb was cute.

"Check once you're seated." Khloe placed her tray on a table for four next to a window facing the tennis courts. I set my tray across from her.

"Thanks," I said. "I def didn't want Drew to see me in a cute outfit covered with cheese and apple pie."

Khloe smiled, flashing the signature beyond-happy smile that I loved. "Just fulfilling my role as new best friend and roomie. Plus, I have to, you know, live with you. I can't have the sitcom moment happen where Teen

Girl spills food on herself in front of Crush."

"Oh? And that impacts you how?" I took a bite of the ultracheesy macaroni, smiling.

Khloe leaned back in her chair, precariously balancing it on its back legs before setting it back down. "Oh, new Canterwood girl. It's roommate code. What one roomie does reflects on the other. If you'd, say, tripped just then, it would have been like *me* tripping."

"Really?" I loved playing with Khloe and hearing her wild ideas.

"*Really.* Your near macaroni stains are my near macaroni stains."

I couldn't help it—I giggled. Khloe shot me a *death slash this really is funny* look. She stuck her nose in the air and took a dainty sip of her soda.

"I certainly don't want to be a bad roommate. I'll look that up in the handbook tonight," I said.

Khloe gave me a satisfied smile. "And my job here is done."

We both burst into giggles. Looking at Khloe, smiling and laughing with me, I couldn't believe how off base I'd been. *This* was perfect, and our friendship was getting better by the day. I needed to stop going back over things and take in the present.

"How's *Beauty and the Beast* going?" I asked.

"Really well," Khloe said. "I checked out a bunch of different versions of the book from the library, did some Internet reading on Mrs. Potts, and have been hitting my lines during rehearsal."

"I'm so proud of you. I can't wait to see the performance. How many nights will it run?"

"Four," Khloe said. "It starts just before Thanksgiving break."

"When tickets are for sale, tell me," I said. "I'm coming to every show."

Khloe dropped her fork. Her brown eyes widened and she stared at me. "Lauren. Oh, my God. No." She shook her head. "No way. It's a big enough deal that you're coming to one. You so don't have to do that!"

"I know," I said. "No one's making me. I want to support my bestie and roomie. You're going to steal the show and I wouldn't miss one night."

Khloe looked down at her tray. She didn't say a word. *Not* Khloe Kinsella—like behavior. Khloe always had something to say.

"Khlo?" I reached across the table and touched her elbow. "I didn't think to ask. Is it okay with you that I come? I'm sorry if I just assumed . . ."

Khloe met my eyes and, for the first time since I'd met her, Khloe's eyes were pink. "No, no. Laur, I want you there. It means . . . you have no idea how much it means to me. I was thrilled that you were coming on opening night, but with you being there for every performance—no one's ever done that for me."

I wanted to hug her. "Oh, Khlo. It's not just about being there for support. I want you to know how seriously I take your acting career. No matter what role you have in this play and future ones, I'm coming to *all* of the performances. I'll be handing out flyers in all of my classes and telling everyone that *my* roommate, an incredibly talented actress, is onstage and they better see her before she hits LA or New York City."

A tear dripped onto Khloe's tray. Quickly, she brushed her cheek with her hand. Supporting her was more important than I'd realized. When I'd first met Lexa and she'd given me the lowdown on Khloe, she'd told me that Khloe *never* cried.

"Hey," I said, taking her hand. "I don't say things I don't mean. I want to help you every step with this. I'm no actress, but I'll run lines, practice blocking with you—whatever you need."

Khloe squeezed my hand. "You're the best. I've never

had a friend take my acting this seriously." She wiped her cheek again, smiling. "Now I *really* want to impress you on stage."

"I'm not worried. I know you'll kill it."

"I'm definitely taking you up on the offer for help," Khloe said. "I'd love to practice with you. And, if there's anything I can do in return, tell me and it's done."

We let go of each other's hands and I picked up my sandwich. "I'll let you know. It may be tracking down Drew."

We fell into an easy chatter, eating and ignoring the other students. I forgot about time and future classes and let myself fall into my conversation with Khloe.

"Wait, wait," I said, holding up a hand. "Clare told you *what* last night?"

Khloe looked over my shoulder. "Checking to be sure Riley hadn't sneaked closer," she explained. "Clare said that Riley's been talking about you and Red Oak a lot. Apparently, she really feels for you. Like, she connected with you sharing something big since she shared her secret about Toby."

I shook my head. "Not totally buying it. You?"

"Not for a second." Khloe ate the last bite of her sandwich. "I think Riley's popularity—what little she had—is sinking. Not many people ever liked her. She only thought they did because they hung out with her. But it was because of fear. Riley sees you as this girl who stepped in to Canterwood, was immediately popular, and has this stellar riding background."

"And?" I was confused.

"And she wants to keep her public snark at you to a minimum so people assume you guys are friends. It'll make her popular by association. Maybe she thinks you'll forgive and forget."

I took a sip of water. "Not happening. She's crazy if she thinks I'm going to become best friends with your arch nemesis. Plus, she hated me until she found out about Red Oak."

Before Khloe could respond, three guys slid into Khloe's side of the booth and three stood at the end of our table. They held lunch trays or put them on our table.

"Khloe," the guy sitting next to her said. "Now we know where you've been. Hanging out with your cute new roomie. Way to hold out on us."

"Shawn!" Khloe shoved his arm, giggling. "Way to barge into a conversation."

Shawn and the other guys smiled at me.

"Going to introduce her, or do we have to guess her

name?" one of the guys who stood asked. He had a mass of dark curls.

Khloe shook her head. "Right. Sorry. Guys, this is Lauren Towers. Lauren, these are my friends . . ."

Khloe stopped short of introducing them. Their eyes were on her, expectant and waiting.

Shawn reached across the table and shook my hand. His honey-brown eyes locked with mine. "I'm Shawn, like Khloe said. These are my friends Michael, Travis, Robb, Todd, and Corey."

"How do you know Khloe?" I asked. I'd seen her wave at some of the guys in the halls, but I didn't know they were friends-friends.

"Can't even remember," Michael said, shaking his blond head. "We live in Blackwell, and I think we met Khloe in different classes last year. She's like an honorary member of Blackwell."

Across the table talkative Khloe from minutes earlier was silent. She was focused on her tray, moving around the last bite of apple pie. If these guys were her friends, why hadn't she mentioned me at *all*?

"Cool," I said. "Khloe and I are *really* good friends. If it weren't for her, I wouldn't know how to do anything at Canterwood. She's taught me everything I know."

I waited for Khloe to interject. Maybe she'd tell them the story of how she'd introduced herself to me. That was a Khloe classic.

"Oh, yeah?" Shawn asked, his green-gray eyes on my face. "Khloe's good about that stuff. If she's not available sometime, I'd be happy to help you."

"Thanks," I said.

"Where are you from?" Michael asked, leaning on the table and plucking a chili cheese fry from his plate.

"Union," I said. "I came here for the riding team."

The guys nodded. "I've seen people practicing," Shawn said. "Do you have a horse?"

I smiled. "Her name's Whisper. We do everything, but dressage is my favorite."

"Dressage is like that really fancy one, right?" Michael asked. He took a sip of Khloe's Dr Pepper.

"Yep. You guys into sports?" If they were Khloe's friends, I wanted to get to know them. I couldn't have expected her to have told every person she knew about me.

Each guy nodded. Most replied with football, basketball, or lacrosse.

I looked at Khloe, who was still quiet. She pushed a button on her phone. "Sorry, guys. I've got to bail. The bell's going to ring any second."

"I'll come with you," I said. "I'm done."

"That's okay." Khloe stood, and the boys moved out of her way. "I forgot that I have to catch Riley and ask her some stuff about the play."

"Oh. Okay. BBM you later."

Khloe flashed me and the guys a smile. "Later."

Since we had the same lunch period, we always left together. The guys settled into our booth and started eating their lunches, continuing their line of questions. They were all nice, but Khloe had just bolted, leaving me with guys I didn't know. Guys I'd have to excuse myself in front of two seconds after Khloe had left.

"Nice to meet you, guys," I said. "I'm going to pull the lame-but-true card and head to class so I'm not late."

"We'll give you a pass this time," Shawn said. The rest of the guys smiled. I gathered my stuff and left, passing Riley's empty table.

Once I was outside of the caf, I took a breath. *What* had just happened? If Khloe had an upcoming convo with Riley, we totally would have mocked it all through lunch. There's no way she could have forgotten about it. Something didn't feel right. Sure, it really wasn't realistic to expect Khloe to introduce me to every person she knew at Canterwood. But those guys seemed like fairly close friends. I hadn't come up *once*? Not even, "Oh, I got a new roommate named Lauren." Those guys hadn't even known my name.

I typed a BBM to Lexa.

Lauren:

Want 2 groom/tack up 2gether b4 lesson?

I reached Mme. Lafleur's French class when my phone vibrated.

Lexa:

Totally! ☺ *Know ur @ French so "Good luck" however the French say it, lol.*

I smiled and walked into class, sitting a few seats away from Riley. The *Beauty and the Beast* script was open on her desk, her lines highlighted. Her French book? Nowhere in sight.

My phone buzzed. I reached down to turn it off. Mme. Lafleur had batlike sonic hearing. But she wasn't here yet. I opened BBM and there was a message from Riley.

Riley:

Bonjour! Sry I had to steal ur bestie aftr lunch. But it looked like u had plenty of company.

Lauren:

No big. Those were K's friends. I heard the play's going well.

I wanted to change the subject, and I knew she'd talk

endlessly about herself and the play until I could wriggle out of the convo.

Riley:

OH—the play is awesome! Mr. Barber thinks this could be THE play that gets me noticed.

Lauren:

Cool. I heard ur all working hard, so GL.

Mme. Lafleur walked, rather *glided*, into the room and sat at her desk. She looked elegant—her shiny brown hair in a chignon and her gray-green eyes lightly rimmed with kohl. She didn't take attendance every day. So, if we decided to skip class, it was a gamble if we'd get caught or not. Today she put her attendance book aside.

"*Bonjour,*" Mme. Lafleur said.

"*Bonjour, Madame Lafleur,*" we responded.

"Today, we're going to start on page twenty-four in your textbook. Please open to that page and take out a notebook and pen."

I did as instructed and didn't glance in Riley's direction. The drama outside the classroom slipped from my mind as I focused on French. I truly loved the language. It was romantic and beautiful. I daydreamed about being fluent and traveling to Paris as a college fashion intern. I envisioned eating an almond croissant at a tiny café, grabbing coffee to go, and walking into an office at Chanel.

Stop, Lauren! Geez! I scolded myself. If I let myself go as far as thinking about clothes, I'd never get my attention back.

I turned to page twenty-four and became absorbed by the lesson. Mme. Lafleur talked with us about how many different countries spoke French and how each of those had their own take on the language. If I paid attention now, it would all be worth it if I ever applied for my dream internship.

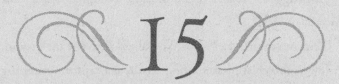

15

TRUST YOUR GUT

LEXA AND I BUMPED INTO EACH OTHER ON the way to the stable. She looked sleek, with black breeches tucked into shiny black boots and a rust-colored shirt with satin ruching on the neckline.

"Nice timing, LT," Lexa said.

"You too," I said. "Want to grab Honor and Whisper and meet somewhere to groom and tack up?"

"Want to tie them to their stalls?"

Whisper and Ever were neighbors near the end of the aisle. I rubbed my palms on my dark fawn-colored breeches. "Can we go somewhere private? Quieter?"

Lexa pressed her lips together. "Of course. I know a good place. You okay?"

I shrugged. "Yeah. No. I don't know. That's why I want to talk to you."

"Say no more," Lex said. We walked into the tack room. A few younger students stood inside on tiptoes grabbing bridles off racks. Lex and I gathered our horses' tack and left the room. We reached Honor's stall first. The beautiful strawberry roan mare had a wide blaze and four white socks. Thanks to Lexa's meticulous grooming, every white hair on Honor's body sparkled. Always.

We took our grooming kits out of our tack trunks and put everything on the lids. I plucked Whisper's baby blue cotton lead line off the hook near her stall door.

"Hi, girly," I said, my voice soft. I peered into the stall, not wanting to barge in and startle her. Whisper faced the stall door, a hind leg cocked as she rested. She pointed both ears forward at the sound of my voice. I grinned, opening the door. Whisper walked to me, her dark eyes soft. She breathed on my palms as I ran my hands over her muzzle. It felt like velvet.

"Pretty girl," I said. I kissed her muzzle and reached to scratch under her forelock. Tiny gray hairs fell to the bed of sawdust beneath us. "Not that you're already not gorgeous enough, but how about we go with Lex and Honor? You deserve a special grooming before our lesson."

Whisper let out a low, barely audible nicker. "I'll take that as a yes."

I snapped the lead line to the gold ring under her chin and led her out. Mimicking Lexa, I put Whisper's saddle pad, saddle, and bridle onto her back and laid the girth on the top. I picked up her sky blue plastic grooming kit with my free hand.

"This way," Lex said. Honor swished her tail—content—and looked pretty in a plum-colored halter.

Whisper and I followed them down the stable aisle. Students were everywhere. Most of the crossties had been filled and everyone was busy. One older boy trimmed a bay's bridle path with whirring Wahl clippers. Another guy was bent over a chestnut's hind leg with a hoof pick. A couple of girls had tied their horses close together, laughing as they groomed them.

We passed Ever's stall. Khloe's bay Hanoverian mare was asleep in the back of her stall. Khloe's advanced lesson wasn't until after mine and Lexa's.

We exited the stable and walked the horses over to a dirt patch with tie rings. It was away from stable noises but close enough that we wouldn't have to rush to get back.

"This okay?" Lexa asked.

"Perfect," I said. "We have a great view."

We looked in front of us. Dark wooden fences kept dozens of turned out horses from wandering onto campus. Open bales of hay gleamed a dusty yellow against the green grass. Most horses grazed, but a couple cantered in playful circles, nipping at each other.

Whisper and Honor pricked their ears at the sounds of the playful horses. Honor's entire body shook as she let out a trumpeting neigh. One of the horses called back.

"No," Lexa said. She gave a quick tug on Honor's lead line. "We're not going to play."

Honor kept her ears in the direction of the horses but stayed quiet. I tied Whisper with a slipknot to her tie ring. Her head was as high as Honor's, watching the other horses, but she hadn't made a sound. I patted her shoulder, reinforcing her good behavior.

We took off the tack, setting it on nearby stands, and dug into our grooming kits. I pulled out my stiff dandy brush. "Did you roll during your turnout?" I asked Whisper. She blinked her big brown eyes at me, flashing her curly lashes. "That doesn't make you look innocent," I teased. Dirt along her poll and tangles in her mane gave her away.

Lexa laughed. "I always ask Honor the same thing

when she rolls before a lesson. She had the most *awful* grass stains once on her blaze and I was like, 'Honor! How *did* you do that?'"

We giggled. The horses settled as we fell into the familiar grooming routine.

Lexa cleared her throat. "So, I know you didn't ask me to go somewhere private just because. What's up, LT?"

I brushed a stubborn dirt clump on Whisper's foreleg. "Something weird happened with Khloe at lunch. I'm *sure* I'm overthinking things and being sensitive, but my feelings got kind of hurt."

Lexa peered at me over Honor's back. "What happened?"

"Khloe and I were having a really fun lunch. We talked about Drew and Zack and lots of stuff. Then these guys came up to us. Boys that I've seen Khloe say hi to or wave at in the hallway, but they sat by her and were definitely friends. Not acquaintances, like I'd thought."

"Names?" Lex asked. She bent over Honor's right front hoof.

"Shawn was sort of the leader. He asked Khloe why she'd been holding out from introducing her 'cute new roommate' to him. None of them knew my name. They were really nice and friendly. I didn't get why Khloe wouldn't have said *something* to them—as her friends— that she had a new roommate."

Lexa released Honor's hoof and moved to pick the mare's back hoof. "That would have hurt my feelings, too," she said. "But Khloe also has a *ton* of 'friends,' aka people who know her and act like they're superclose but only talk to her every once in a while. It's totally possible that Khlo hadn't had a convo with them since school started. Maybe they were acting like they were Khloe's BFFs to impress you."

"Why? They didn't even know me. They just found out I existed at lunch."

"Maybe they've seen you in the hallway and never came up to you. Our grade is fairly small. Old students notice new ones and, like that guy said, you've already made a name for yourself here."

Everyone kept saying that, but it didn't feel like it. I was just being myself. I wasn't trying to win a popularity contest.

"What if Khloe *did* hang out with them recently and didn't say anything?" I asked.

Lexa stood, resting her arms on Honor's back. "It's possible, but it wouldn't be malicious. Khloe might have said hi to those guys in passing and that was all. It's also only the second week of school and there are a zillion 'catch up' convos—you know how those go. So, maybe she *did* talk with them, but it slipped her mind."

I took a breath, inhaling Whisper's sweet scent—hay and slightly floral—and processed what Lexa had said.

"Thanks, Lex," I said. "I know you're right. Khloe's not like that. I guess I just needed to hear it from someone else."

"Understandable."

Lexa smiled at me and picked up Honor's body brush. I worked the dirt out of Wisp's coat and switched to a smoother brush. Lexa had made me feel better about Shawn and the other guys. I felt silly for thinking Khloe had ditched me at lunch. I definitely was *not* bringing that up with Lex. I wanted to leave it at that. Plus, I had to remember that Khloe was also Lexa's best friend. I never wanted to put Lexa in an uncomfortable position by coming to her with questions about Khloe's motives. I needed to trust my gut more often.

16

WHISPER + LT = HARMONY

"WELCOME, CLASS," MR. CONNER SAID. MY class of six had gathered our horses in front of him in the indoor arena. We were warmed up and waiting for instruction. I kept my gaze straight ahead, not allowing myself to glance to my right.

Drew was next to me on Polo. *Très* exciting! He'd ridden up to Lexa and me when we'd entered the arena. Lexa, not so subtly, had left to chat with Cole. Drew and I had warmed up our horses side by side, talking about our day. He looked irresistibly cute in a waffle-knit dark gray shirt and black breeches. Polo, his blood bay gelding, stood still next to Whisper.

". . . that's why I want to focus on assessing you and your horse's dressage skill level," Mr. Conner said.

Oops.

"I want to talk a little about dressage and ask you questions," Mr. Conner continued. He slowly walked back and forth in front of us. He wore his usual hunter green polo with the gold CCA logo stitched a couple of inches below his collar.

"Dressage is a vital training area to each of you because it develops subtle aids, soft hands, and a balanced seat, among other things," he said. "For your horse, it helps with stiff movements, suppleness, and strength. The goal of our dressage work will be to unite you and your horse as one and a long-lasting team. Harmony is the goal."

We nodded, and Mr. Conner's eyes stopped on Clare. "Clare, why are stiff movements a problem?"

"It can create injury if a horse moves incorrectly," Clare answered easily. "It also makes it harder on the rider."

Mr. Conner nodded. "Well said. If we're striving for engagement from the horse, Cole, what two types are we seeking?"

A couple horses down, Cole looked at Mr. Conner. "Proper tucking and swinging," he said.

Dressage talk made me *so* happy! This was my world. I could discuss dressage forever.

"Lauren," Mr. Conner said, walking toward Whisper and me. "Can you explain tucking and swinging?"

"Yes," I said. "In its correct form, tucking is when a horse tucks his hindquarters, flexing and bending the joints of his hind legs. A horse should tuck when he's asked for a collected gait, rebalancing, or . . ." I blanked on the last one.

"Downward transitions," Mr. Conner added, smiling.

"Yes, thank you." I tried not to get flustered. "And swinging is also about the hindquarters. It's when a horse swings the hind legs forward and takes a long stride. There's not much flexing. This makes it easier for the horse to propel forward."

Mr. Conner tipped his head to me. "Excellent. Thank you. Okay, who can tell me the types of correct walk in dressage?"

"Working, collected, medium, free, extended," Drew answered.

Mr. Conner quizzed us with the same question for trotting and cantering.

"Take your horses to the wall and space them out," Mr. Conner said once we'd finished his questions. "We're going to take the horses through each of the types of walking, trotting, and cantering you've described. We'll stop after each gait and talk about any problem areas."

We rode to the wall, and I fell behind Drew and in front of Lexa.

"Please begin a free walk," Mr. Conner said. "Remember this is a four-beat gait with no suspension."

I eased up on the reins, giving Whisper room to move her head and neck. Her strides were long and they covered the ground—perfect for a free walk.

"Loosen your reins, Cole," Mr. Conner called.

Mr. Conner watched us for a few minutes. "Good," he called. "Switch to a working walk."

I tightened the reins slightly but let Whisper move freely. I pressed my calves gently against her side and she moved forward, almost breaking into a trot.

"Not so much pressure, Lauren," Mr. Conner said. "I want to see Whisper energetic, but not pushing for a trot."

I took his cues and Whisper settled into a working walk with even steps.

We moved through the other types of walking and switched to a trot. Whisper's ears flicked back and forth. She'd been testing me during the last round of walking. She wanted to go faster.

"As a reminder, the trot is a two-beat gait," Mr. Conner said from the center of the arena. His eyes shifted from pair to pair. "The horse moves from one diagonal pair of legs to the next, and there should be suspension in between. While we go through the types of trots, I want to see elasticity, steadiness, engaged hindquarters, and a rounded back. Please begin a collected trot."

I let out a little rein and cued Whisper to execute a collected trot. She moved forward with short steps, lifting her legs higher as she settled into the faster gait.

"Nice, everyone," Mr. Conner called.

Whisper stretched her neck, wanting to catch Polo. She shifted her weight and leaned against the bit. Each step was faster and her strides became irregular. Posting to the bumpy trot wasn't easy.

I pulled her to a walk and started over. *You and Whisper have* only *been working together since this summer,* I reminded myself. *You've got a lot to teach her.* It wasn't fair to expect Whisper to be as experienced as some of the dressage veterans I'd ridden in competition.

Lexa trotted Honor past us and I checked Whisper to keep her from taking off after them. Her muscles bunched beneath me and her ears flattened, unhappy with my decision. I kept Whisper at a walk until we'd fallen behind Riley, the last in line, before asking for a collected trot again.

This time, Whisper maintained the same pace and kept

her neck high and arched. She pushed forward with her hindquarters and was on the bit instead of leaning on it.

"Good work, Lauren," Mr. Conner called. "Whisper looks light on her forehand. Beautiful."

I didn't let his compliment derail my attention to Whisper. Almost as if she'd been embarrassed by being forced to the back of the line, Whisper moved like an angel through the rest of the trotting exercises. I felt more in tune with her than I ever had. Dressage was what made me feel alive. Completing the movements correctly with Whisper felt like heaven.

Everyone else seemed to have a fairly easy time with the exercise. Mr. Conner commented throughout, but they were all quick corrections. The other five horses—Polo, Valentino, Honor, Fuego, and Adonis—trotted musically along the arena wall.

"Last part," Mr. Conner said. "Let's work on cantering. I should *not* have to tell you by now that this is a three-beat gait. We're working on cantering to help balance, roundness, forward movement, and impulsion. Keep your mount's hindquarters engaged and supple."

Mr. Conner asked us for a collected canter and, without incident, the horses completed each command. Whisper shook out her main during the extended canter. She loved lengthening her stride to the fullest. I stayed prepared for her to lean on the bit or become excited from cantering with other horses, but she remained calm.

"Riley," Mr. Conner called. "Adonis's canter became hollow a few strides back."

I looked across the arena at Riley, and I couldn't see her cues to Adonis. I wondered if she'd even decided to correct his movement. I'd barely finished my thought when Adonis's back rounded and his canter turned light and steady. Riley was talented.

After another lap around the arena, Mr. Conner raised his hand. "Please draw your horses to a walk."

Whisper and the rest of the horses breathed a little faster than normal. A line of sweat trickled from beneath Polo's red saddle pad. The lesson had kept all of the horses and riders physically and mentally engaged. Or Whisper and I, at least.

Mr. Conner let us lap him once at a walk before calling us to the center. "Wonderful work, everyone," he said. "I'm impressed that each of you was able to correct problem areas that were revealed during different gaits. Everyone demonstrated a valuable strength in dressage."

Smiling, I looked at Cole on my left. He smiled back and rubbed Valentino's neck.

"Please make sure your horses are completely cool before putting them away," Mr. Conner said. "I look forward to tomorrow's lesson. Read the next section of your horse manual and be prepared to answer questions. We'll meet in the large outdoor arena."

Mr. Conner exited the arena and each of us dismounted. I loosened Whisper's girth and ran up the stirrup irons.

"You were such a good girl," I said, kissing her muzzle. "I'm so proud of you. You're a dressage star."

I clucked my tongue, urging her forward for a cool down, and someone waved near the entrance. Khloe.

"Hey," I said, leading Whisper to Khloe. Lexa and Honor were a few strides behind us.

"I tacked up early, and Ever and I caught the last few minutes of your lesson," Khloe said. She scuffed a boot in the dirt. "I wasn't spying, I swear."

"I don't mind if you watch," I said.

"Hey," Lex said, reaching us. She high-fived Khloe.

"I just told LT that I saw a bit of your lesson," Khloe said. She put on her black helmet, snapping the chin strap. "You guys looked great. Honor and Whisper are such gorgeous movers."

Lexa and I smiled. I'd *never* stop feeling crazy-proud when someone complimented Whisper.

Khloe looked over her shoulder as horseshoes rang down the concrete. "I better go. We're working outside today."

"Good luck," I said.

"Yeah, I'm sure you'll do great," Lex added. She scratched Ever's cheek.

"Thanks, guys," Khloe said. She touched Honor's and Whisper's muzzles. "Oh, Laur. I think we need to have a *serious* talk tonight."

"About what?" I asked. Khloe's tone was scary-serious.

Khloe grinned. "About how much Drew stared at you during your lesson!"

"He was?!" I grinned, both because of the observation and because Khloe's serious act wasn't real.

Lexa bumped my shoulder with hers. "He was, oh blind one."

"Drew likes Lauren! Drew likes Lauren!" Khloe sang.

"KHLOE! Shhhh!" I waved an arm at her. "He. Is. In. Here."

Khloe held back a laugh. "Oops. Sorry, LT."

"Lauren likes Drew!" Lexa whispered.

"Guys! He's going to hear you!" I shot my friends looks, but I was on the verge of laughter too.

The three of us burst into giggles. We didn't even hear the approaching horseshoes.

"Later, guys," Drew said, halting Polo beside us.

Our giggles stopped. Immediately.

"Everything okay?" Drew asked. His blue eyes looked from person to person.

"Fine. Totally fine," Khloe said.

"Oh, yeah. Great!" Lexa added.

"We're so good," I finished.

Oh, mon Dieu! We could *not* have been more awkward.

"Okaaay," Drew said. He shook his head, then led Polo toward the exit.

"Bye!" We simultaneously chirped.

The second he was out of earshot, we collapsed into laughter again.

17

GOT HIS NUMBER

"MY DAD IS *INSANE*," I SAID TO KHLOE. I laughed, holding up my BlackBerry. "He sent me an e-mail to say good morning."

Khloe looked up from where she stood in front of the full-length mirror, curling her hair. Chunks of blond hair were sectioned with clips. "And that's insane how . . . ?"

"Oh," I said. "Because he wrote it in what his version of 'teen slang' is."

"Read it!" Khloe said.

I'd been sitting at my desk doing makeup when my phone had chimed. Khloe and I were both in robes, our outfits laid out on our beds.

"Okay, and envision this in IM style where applicable,"

I said. "He wrote, 'Hey, Laurbell! What's up? How r u & ur roomie? Mom & I miss u x a zillion! We decided 2 turn ur room into storage 4 the antiques we r going 2 buy. Hope u r finding time 2 chillax. Give Wisp a hug. G2G. Write me back! Luv, Dad.'"

Khloe laughed, then paused. "Your parents *do* know you're coming home for breaks and stuff, right? Aren't your feelings hurt that they're turning your room into storage?!"

I rolled my eyes, grinning. "That's my dad being funny. He and my mom hate antiquing. He knows I'm OCD about my room and would *freak* if anything was moved."

"Ohhh." Khloe smiled. "I like your dad and I haven't even met him."

"You'll meet him on Family Day," I reminded her.

Khloe released the clamp of her iron, the final curl cascading down her back. "I can't wait to meet your family. And for you to meet mine!"

Simultaneously, we looked up at the wall clock. We should have been out of Hawthorne five minutes ago.

"Oops!" Khloe said. She turned off the iron; I put down my phone and finished my makeup. I'd done a swipe of shimmery caramel eye shadow with clear glossy lips and a coat of Cover Girl mascara.

Khloe and I got dressed, helping each other with zippers and buttons. I'd paired jeans with a white ribbed tank top under a three-quarters-sleeve pale yellow shirt that I'd borrowed from Khloe. Patent leather ballet flats completed the look.

Khloe's outfit was as wild as mine was subdued. But she pulled it off looking effortlessly cool. She wore a white T-shirt with lime green stitching, a flowy, flirty black skirt, and hot pink peep-toe ballet flats with sequin fabric.

"We need accessories!" Khloe said, looking toward the top of her dresser, where we'd pooled our rings, necklaces, and other jewelry.

"Do you want to wear fab hoops in detention?" I asked. "Let's go!"

Khloe grumbled but grabbed her bag. We swung our backpacks over our shoulders and half-jogged down Hawthorne's empty hallway.

Christina poked her head out of her office as we approached. "I'd say stay and let's have a conversation about why you're late," she said. Her light-brown hair was up in a ponytail. "But you're late. Go."

"Thanks, and sorry!" I said.

Khloe tossed her a smile and we hurried past her and

through the doors. The campus was eerily empty. Wasn't anyone else *ever* late?!

Khloe and I didn't have time to talk as we dashed across the lawn to the English building. We stopped running two steps before Mr. Davidson's open door and walked inside. I glanced at his desk, expecting him to be staring at us. But his seat was empty.

"Sit, sit!" Lexa hissed. Khloe and I slid into seats next to her.

"Where's Mr. Davidson?" I asked, taking jagged breaths. Running across campus with twenty pounds of books wasn't easy!

"He *just* stepped out to grab something from his office," Lexa said. "He's taking attendance when he gets back."

"Niiice!" Khloe said, high-fiving me.

In the next aisle, Garret leaned toward me. "Think I should mention that you and KK just got here?" He grinned teasingly. His cropped red hair looked wet, like he'd just showered before class. Zack sat in front of him and was talking to Khloe, who'd ended up next to him.

"Sure," I said, deadpan. "And I'll pipe right up with how you copied Zack's notes last class instead of taking your own."

Garret put a hand over his heart as if I'd stabbed him. "Ouch. No messing with you, LT."

I grinned. "Not when it comes to detention."

After English, I had a BBM from Brielle.

Brielle:

Srry I couldn't talk yest! So busy w/school. Ugh! Def want 2 catch up soon! Xoxo

I locked my phone and put it in my bag. I really wanted to talk to Brielle, but I understood the busy part.

The rest of my classes flew by. In our room, Khloe and I changed into riding clothes. I realized I was doing everything way faster than usual. Like, I-put-my-paddock-boots-on-the-wrong-feet fast.

"In a rush to see Drew, perhaps?" Khloe asked.

"No argument from me," I said. "I give in. I want to get there to warm up with Drew. Maybe we'll get a chance to talk . . ."

Khloe smiled. "I'm *sure* you'll talk."

Giggling, we got ready for our lessons and, from the time I left our dorm till I got to the stable, I thought about one very cute dark-haired boy with ocean-blue eyes. I wished I could blog about Drew. That would be the best entry ever.

• • •

After riding, I hopped off Whisper, leading her forward. "You were so good, girl," I said. I rubbed her forehead. The lesson had been challenging—Mr. Conner had made my class perform a variety of flatwork exercises. He was definitely upping the degree of difficulty to prepare us for the schooling show. That was something I thought on and off about. One second, it made me panic to even think about entering a show arena. The next, I couldn't wait to show on *my* horse. With everything going on, I'd been too busy to focus on my feelings about the show.

Clare and Riley had already led their horses out of the arena, but I kept Whisper back. "Let them get *far* ahead of us." Whisper bobbed her head, seeming to understand.

"Later, LT," Cole said, leading Valentino past us.

"Yeah, talk later!" Lexa added, with Honor in tow.

I waved to them. Drew was the only one left inside with me. He walked Polo along the wall, letting the gelding stretch.

I undid my chin strap and latched my helmet onto Whisper's saddle. She stood still while I ran up the stirrups. I pretended to struggle with the girth so I could watch Drew. We'd exchanged our usual "hey"s and had talked a little before the lesson. I felt like hanging around for another minute to say good-bye.

I smoothed the ultralight windbreaker that I'd gone back to my room to get after stepping out of Hawthorne for my lesson. The air had gotten unseasonably chilly and I'd added the jacket over my white V-neck tee.

Drew was still along the wall, leading Polo with his helmet tucked under one arm. Now I felt like I'd be interrupting.

I reached under Whisper's chin and took the reins. "C'mon, girl. Let's get you cool and groomed."

We started forward, Whisper's tail swishing lazily as we went toward the exit. "I think you deserve a treat after today," I said. "Maybe an apple? I *might* have brought one from lunch."

I loved feeding Whisper the juicy fruits. She took dainty bites at first, then got excited and munched until apple juice ran down her chin. It always made me laugh when the liquid coated her fine chin whiskers.

"Hey, Laur!"

I halted Whisper, turning to look back. Drew walked Polo in our direction, hurrying a little. The way he said "Laur" made me smile.

"Hi," I said. Drew stopped Polo next to Whisper. The two horses tugged against the reins, stretching their necks toward the other. I gave Whisper more room and let her touch muzzles with Polo. The gelding blew a big breath into her nostrils and the two stood, content.

"Good lesson, huh?" Drew asked.

"Yeah, Mr. Conner's really making us do different things. Classes are never boring."

"Definitely not. I'm waiting, though, for things to get a lot harder. You'll get to see me fly over a jump *without* Polo a couple of times, I'm sure."

I shook my head. "No way. Please. I've seen you during jumping. You guys are tight."

Drew grinned, rubbing the back of his neck. "Tight until we reach an obstacle Polo doesn't like."

I giggled. "Okay. I guess I will keep an eye out for flying Drews."

"What are you doing after this?" Drew asked.

"Glee club practice. I've got to groom Wisp and get her stall ready, then go."

Drew looked at me, his blue eyes intense. "Let me know when you guys are performing. I'll come watch sometime."

I smiled, forcing myself not to blush. "Definitely. I'd like that."

"Do you have your phone?"

I pulled my BlackBerry out of my boot. Khloe had taught me how to clip it inside my tall boots so I could have it on me at the stable.

I held it up. "Yeah?"

"Well, it might be easier for you to tell me about glee if you have my number," Drew said. "Can I put it in your phone?"

"Sure," I said, handing it over. My fingers brushed his and my skin tingled. I hadn't felt like this since Taylor. It almost felt even *stronger* with Drew.

He passed my phone back to me, smiling. I stared at the screen—at his number.

"Thanks," I said. "That *will* make it easier. But no picture?"

"You sure you want *my* face in your address book?" Drew asked.

Very!

I nodded. "One pic."

Drew made a go-ahead motion with his hand. I tried to keep my fingers from shaking as I pushed the camera button and zoomed in on Drew's face. "On three," I said. "One . . . two . . . three!"

I pushed the button and the flash illuminated Drew's face. Drew stepped closer when the camera had finished and I held out my phone so he could see too.

He shook his head, smiling. "*When* you get sick of seeing my face, feel free to replace it with a pic of Polo. He's much more photogenic."

Drew was *ridiculous*. The picture was perfect. His creamy ivory skin looked flawless against his dark hair. Blue eyes seemed to come through the phone screen, and his soft pink lips made his white smile *très parfait*.

I looked up, realizing I'd been staring at my phone. For a while.

"I know you have to get to glee," Drew said. "But text me sometime if you want."

I nodded. "I will. Thanks."

We smiled at each other, and he led Polo out of the indoor arena. I stood there, my feet too heavy to lift, and kept moving the touchpad on my phone to keep the backlight off.

"Um, Lauren?"

"Huh?" My head snapped up. Mike stood in front of me in the doorway. "What?" I almost dropped my phone.

"Another group is coming in soon," Mike said, looking at me, then my phone. "You okay?"

"Totally fine," I said. "Sorry. I got distracted. I'm going."

I followed him out of the arena, wondering if it was possible to groom Whisper, feed her, give her fresh water, and muck her stall all while holding my phone.

18

NO INTRODUCTION
NECESSARY

I REALIZED ON MY WAY TO GLEE CLUB THAT if I spent much more time looking at Drew's pic, my battery would die. In Khloe-speak, what had happened with Drew was "majorly amaze!" I'd texted her the second I'd reached Whisper's stall. She'd responded immediately—she'd just been warming up for her lesson, so she'd checked her phone before Mr. Conner had come into the arena. Khloe was waiting for the play-by-play tonight. I'd also texted Lexa who sent back a ton of *!!!!* and ☺ ☺ ☺. She said she and Cole were studying in the library tonight if I had homework and wanted company. I decided I'd meet them while Khloe had *Beauty and the Beast* rehearsal.

My phone buzzed. Drew had accepted my contact request on BBM! His icon—an electric guitar against a black background—was next to his name in my contacts list among Khloe's, Cole's, Lexa's, and a few other people's. I exited BBM. Then logged back in. His name was still there.

I scrolled to his name, clicked, and typed.

Lauren:

Hey! Had fun talking 2 u 2day. C u tmrw.

I put my phone on silent, knowing I had to focus on glee. My smile wouldn't go away. I took the sidewalk that dipped downhill to the media center. In a "Welcome to Glee Club" e-mail, the faculty advisor, Mr. Harrison, said we'd meet in room 109. The auditorium would be used for special practices and performances.

I followed the door numbers until I reached 109. I opened the door and looked around. The room was perfect! One corner had a set of drums. A baby grand piano was in the other. Music stands were lined up along one wall and a desk had piles of sheet music.

Metal folding chairs were arranged in a circle, and I sat in a red one, my back to the window. It had taken me a little longer than usual at the stable because of my refusal to put down my phone for more than ten seconds. I was surprised to be the only one he—

"Hi, Lauren!"

I jumped. "Melissa! You scared me! I didn't see anyone else in here."

"Sorry!" The other girl smiled, standing up from behind a desk. "I was finishing reorganizing some files. Are you *so* excited about our first glee practice this year?"

Melissa Peeples had been helping Mr. Harrison the day of tryouts. She seemed full of endless energy, and her genuine love of glee made it hard for me *not* to be excited.

"I hope I'm ready," I said. "I'm definitely not going to be the star singer or dancer, but I joined because it's fun."

Melissa flitted around the room like a hummingbird. Her blue skirt swished above her knees and looked *très* chic with her black ballet flats with tiny bows. "You'll be great," she said, brushing her long brown hair over one shoulder. "We're a group—Mr. Harrison makes sure we stay that way. No divas allowed."

Three girls, one I recognized from Hawthorne, walked in together. They smiled at me and took seats in the circle.

"Hi, Lauren," one of the girls said. Her platinum-blond hair was back in two loose French braids.

"Hey, Carlee." *Whew.* Her name came to me just in time. Carlee lived in Orchard, but we had science together.

More people filled the room, and Melissa said a cheerful "hello!" to everyone who walked in.

Cole entered, wearing breeches like mine. He practically pounced on the seat next to me and stared at me with wide eyes.

"What?" I asked, laughing. "Why are you looking at me like that?"

Cole folded his arms. "Ah, you're playing the I'm-so-coy game. Not today. Not for this! Lauren, Lexa told me!"

I turned toward him. I'd been planning to try and wait until after glee club to talk about it, but if Lexa already told him . . .

"Drew gave me his number!" I whisper-shouted. "He put it in my phone and then I took his picture."

"How did you even have the guts to ask for the pic?" Cole slipped out of his black cardigan. "I would have practically died after getting his number."

"I don't know. I just *did*. It was scary and exciting, then it was easy and things felt cool between us. Like I could ask him for the pic and not be scared." I felt my phone, now in my jacket pocket. It almost felt hot through my clothes. "Want to see?"

"Um, *yes!*" Cole said.

Laughing, I took out my phone and showed him Drew's name. Cole grinned. "So, he likes music, huh?"

"I'm thinking the guitar icon means *yes*, but that's

something I'll just have to find out." I pocketed the phone just as Mr. Harrison walked into the room. The young teacher closed the door, smiling at us. I counted four guys and six other girls in the seats. Mr. Harrison picked up a handful of papers and sat in the remaining empty chair. He almost looked like an older version of Cole, with his light brown hair and green eyes.

"Hello, everyone," Mr. Harrison said. "Welcome to the first meeting of this year's seventh grade glee club. I'm excited for the year to begin. I can't wait to work with each of you. Some I'll get to know better"—Melissa smiled—"and some, I'll get to know." I smiled at that.

"Today, we'll run through some basic vocal warm-ups, but comfort is something I want to work on first," Mr. Harrison continued. "Not only comfort with yourself in glee and your performing abilities, but your comfort level with one another. That's why I'd like you all to stand and spend some time introducing yourself to all of the people you don't know. We'll warm up when everyone's finished."

Cole and I got up and stepped in front of our chairs. A tall guy with freckles walked up to me. "Hey," he said, putting his hands in his jeans pockets. "I'm Owen. You're Lauren, right?"

"Right," I said. "I'm so sorry to be rude, but do we

have a class together? You knew my name, and I'm sorry that I didn't know yours."

"No classes together," Owen said. "I'm friends with Garret. You have a class with him."

"Oh, yeah. English class."

"What's your favorite kind of music?" Owen asked.

I started to answer, but was hung up on why *Garret* was talking about me. I snapped out of it and answered Owen's question, then asked him the same. After a few more, we moved on to different people. I approached a dark-haired girl with thick bangs and started the whole process all over again.

By the time we finished introductions, my voice was almost worn out from talking. Mr. Harrison started us on some basic warm-up exercises. Melissa's voice rang clear until the final note.

19

NO-SLEEP ZONE

"LET ME SEE!" AN EXCITED KHLOE LUNGED for my phone the second I started to put it on my desk.

I laughed. "You're, like, the tenth person to ask me that today."

"Criminal that I wasn't there to witness it," Khloe said, shaking her head. She picked it up after I plugged it into the charger.

"It so was," I said. "Drew could have been more courteous and waited until you were around to give me his number."

Khloe was too engaged in looking at my BBM to pick up on my joking tone. "He *should* have been. I'll have to talk to him about his timing. He cannot ask my roomie such awesome questions when I'm not there!"

Khloe put down my phone, winking.

"Well, I guess it's a tradeoff, 'cause I missed Zack asking you out," I said. "Even though I technically was here."

"Snoring, but here," Khloe said, smiling.

I washed up in our bathroom and changed into yoga pants and a snug tee. Khloe had books spread on her bed and Watch!—our fave network—on low in the background.

"You've got play rehearsal tonight, right?" I asked. I sank into my chair and started taking out books for homework.

"Yep. I have to leave soon. It's going to be Riley-in-my-face day because she's got a big scene to work on." Khloe stuck out her tongue.

"Sorry," I said. "Remember something, though."

Khloe put her pencil in the middle of her math book. "I'm listening."

"*You're* the girl who has a date on Friday. You're also the girl who's getting a jam-packed facial-slash-hair-slash-mani-pedi session before her date comes."

Khloe grinned, flipping her blond hair back. "I can *so* work with that! Just . . . *eeeee*! Can you believe I'm going out with *Zack*?"

"Yes! You're funny, pretty, silly, smart—he's going to have an amazing time and so are you."

"I can't wait to do our hair, and I've been dreaming about a cucumber mask," Khloe said. "You're going to look even prettier for Drew. You know, the boy in your contact list."

I resisted the urge to look at his name again. "A little maintenance is def needed. Everything's been so crazy. I'm lucky I've had time to condition my hair." I'd been wanting to blog, too, but there had been no time.

Khloe stretched, getting off her bed. "Tell me about it. I always forget how much work fall musicals are until I'm in the middle of one."

"At least we'll smell pretty while we work all weekend," I said, shaking my head.

Khloe, who'd been looking at her phone, tossed it in the black sequin messenger bag that she used for theater. "I totally forgot," she said. "Jill just BBMed me to ask if I'd heard anything about the list."

"The list? What's that?"

"It comes out on Friday. It started last year, I think, by some anonymous students. Or a student. I don't know. Anyway, someone in each grade e-mails a list with the year's 'potentials.'"

I stopped unloading my books. This was way too interesting.

"The list has a bunch of categories," Khloe continued. She stuffed a book in her bag. "Like, Most Likely to Have a Hot Date at Homecoming or Most Potential to Get Caught Sneaking Out. Silly topics like that and some serious categories like class president—that kind of stuff."

Khloe checked the time and snapped her bag shut.

"Did you make 'the list' last year?"

She shouldered her bag, a thin smile on her face. "Yep. Most Likely to Wear the Best Outfit."

"Um, *wow*! Khlo, that's cool!"

"It would have been," Khloe said, nearing the door. "Except Most Potential for Lead Roles went to Riley."

I winced. "I'm sorry."

Khloe opened our door. "Me too. But we'll see who's on the list this year!" She waved and let the door shut softly behind her.

Almost an hour later, I was in the library elevator. A heavy bag of books was in one hand and a travel mug of hot vanilla black tea was in the other. I was so sleepy; I'd almost considered coffee for half a second. I got off on the fifth floor, where Lexa had told me a bunch of people were studying.

I walked past rows of books until I reached the floor's

study area. Lexa, Cole, and Clare were together at the end of a long table. A bunch of people I didn't know were spread out in the other chairs. Most were in groups, but some were solo with earbuds in.

I pulled out a chair across from Clare and put down my mug.

"Hey," I said.

They greeted me back.

"Glad you're here," Lexa said. "Now I can see your face in person when I say . . . Drew gave you his number!"

I blushed. "Lex!" I hissed as Cole and Clare giggled.

"C'mon, Laur! Tell me everything," Lexa said. "I can't believe I was *right there* and I missed it by seconds."

Clare nodded, making her red curls bounce. "You're *so* lucky! Drew's so cute. Every girl is, like, in love with him."

"He's definitely cute," I said. "But we just traded numbers."

"Just?" Clare wrinkled her nose. "I think not."

We laughed quietly. I took out my math book and notebook when I spotted a librarian patrolling the room. I didn't want to get kicked out of the library. Everyone else hunched over their books until the librarian disappeared.

"Riley at rehearsal too?" I asked Clare.

Clare nodded. "Yep. She's been practicing like crazy. I

have to wear headphones when I'm studying in our room or I actually start to write whatever lines she's running!"

"Totally understand," I said, smiling at her. "Khloe's taken the whole 'singing in the shower' thing to the next level." I realized that I liked hanging out with Clare when Riley wasn't around. Clare acted like a different person— someone I could see as Khloe's friend.

"Riley's practicing even more because of next weekend," Clare said. She blew out a breath, running her fingers through her curls.

"What's next weekend?" Lexa asked.

I stayed quiet, watching the interaction between them. Clare and Lexa's relationship was complicated. Lexa was Khloe's BFF, but she and Riley were far from friends. This was one of the few times I'd seen Lex and Clare have a conversation.

"Riley's going to New York City next week," Clare said. "She's staying with her aunt because she got a call-back for a pilot."

"*What?!*" I said. "A callback? When did she audition? And where?"

"Riley not saying anything about an audition seems weird," Cole said. "C'mon, Clare, even you can admit it's odd that she didn't brag about this."

Clare narrowed her eyes, bristling a bit a Cole's comment. "Yes," she finally said. "Riley usually tells people when she has something big going on, but she thinks this gig is a longshot, so she didn't tell many people."

There was no way Khloe knew about this. Her reaction wasn't going to be exactly joyful when I told her. Not when she already had this thing with Riley.

"She didn't leave campus," Clare continued. "She sent in an audition reel she'd made over the summer. Now, I guess the casting directors want to see her in person."

Lexa and Cole asked more questions, but I zoned out. I'd learned all of the vital stuff about Riley's weekend away. Plus, the pile of homework in front of me needed to get smaller. ASAP.

"Hey, hey," Jill said, appearing. "Did I miss quality studying time?"

We all welcomed her.

"Nope," I said. "You missed the good gossip, though."

Jill frowned. "I'll be asking you for the deets later, Lex," she said to her roommate.

I glanced at Jill, knowing *this* was the time to ask about the DVD. I'd put off asking her because I didn't want to stir the now-quiet pot, but I *had* to know. Jill pulled a chair next to me; everyone else had gone back to work.

"Jill," I said quietly. "Can I ask you something?"

She nodded. "Sure. What's up?"

"The morning of the sleepover, was there *any* time that Riley was alone with the DVDs?" I made sure to keep my voice low so Clare didn't hear. "Like, could she have arranged it so you'd choose the DVD somehow?"

Jill shook her head. "It's totally my freaky luck's fault. I picked up a random stack of DVDs, went through them, and picked the one with your show. We were all in the room together, and Riley didn't have access to the DVDs."

"It's *not* your fault," I said. "It was just something I'd been thinking about and had to ask. Plus, Khloe only said it once, but I think she believes Riley planted the DVD."

Lexa, catching some of my sentence, leaned in. "You know Riley and Khloe have a messy past. It totally makes sense that Khloe would, well, *hope* that Riley did this. Then Khloe would finally be able to get revenge for last year."

"What's last year?" I asked.

Lexa glanced around, but no one else at the table was paying attention to us. "Last year, Riley was the one to give Khloe directions to the audition room for the fall musical. Khloe had missed the announcement, so she took Riley's word."

Jill shook her head. "Khloe and Riley didn't know each

other yet, so poor Khlo had no way of knowing that Riley gave her the wrong directions."

"Oh, no!" I said.

"Riley told Khloe the auditions were in the gym because the theater was being renovated," Lexa said, clicking her pen shut. "By the time Khloe figured it out and made it back to the theater, the signup sheet was full and she missed her chance."

"Khloe hasn't forgiven Riley since," Jill said. She pushed up her glasses. "Not like I would, either."

"Poor Khlo. I know she was really hoping Riley had messed with my DVD."

"Believe me," Lexa said, leaning over. "Khloe will get a chance to exact her revenge. Trust me."

With that, we traded nervous looks and got to work.

"Lauren? Laur?"

Someone touched my arm. "What?" I asked, blinking. Lexa stood next to me, her backpack on the table. Everyone else was gone. "Where did Cole and Clare go?" I asked.

Lexa sat down. "You passed out a while ago. You were sound asleep and none of us felt like waking you up was the right thing to do."

"What? No, no, I finished math and . . ." I shook my

head, confused. I glanced down at the notebook in front of me. Nine problems were done. Nine. Out of thirty. I hadn't touched my other homework. "Omigod."

I pressed a button on my phone, checking the time: 8:56.

"I'm sorry, Lauren. The library's closing at nine, so I had to wake you." Lexa opened her mouth and closed it.

"Don't apologize, Lex," I said, slamming my math book. "It's my fault that I fell asleep. I would have done the same thing if I'd been you."

I smiled, not wanting her to feel bad. Inside, I was seething. Not at Lexa, though, at myself. When I'd fallen asleep doing homework before, at least it had been in my room with Khloe. Falling asleep in front of my other friends at the *library* was ridiculous. I kept up a steady chatter with Lexa as we took the elevator downstairs, not wanting her to try to make me feel better.

We started back to Hawthorne. The dark campus was almost empty—lights glowed from dorm halls and cast yellow shadows on the lawn.

"Is everything really okay?" Lexa asked.

"Yeah," I said lightly. "Like what?"

"Just wondering about classes and homework. Khlo said you were up all night a few times working."

I didn't want Lexa to think I couldn't keep up. That sounded like I couldn't handle *Canterwood*. It had been Khloe and Lexa's biggest worry for me, and I'd promised a thousand times that I could handle everything I'd set up for myself at Canterwood. I'd chosen each class, pushed to take advanced courses, and hadn't doubted that I could juggle everything. Until recently. Until I'd gotten a bad grade. Until I'd fallen asleep doing homework in my room. Until I'd fallen asleep in the library.

"Classes are okay," I said. "I fell asleep because math was *so* boring." I smiled, elbowing Lexa.

"Uh-huh," she said. "I'm not going to give you the same 'slow down' speech, but I will say that I hope things ease up soon. Wouldn't want you snoozing in front of Drew."

We passed a black lantern, the gaslit flame flickering and allowing me to catch Lex's grin.

"Nice. Thanks," I said teasingly. "Maybe he thinks snoring is cute."

Lexa pulled open the door to Hawthorne and we squeaked inside just before curfew.

"Add a little drool and Drew will ask you out *for sure*." Lexa grinned, sticking her tongue out at me.

I shook my head and sped up, getting steps ahead of Lex.

"Good night, Lexa!" I called. I opened my door and stuck my tongue out back at her.

Inside, the lights were on and Khloe, standing with her script in hand, stood near her bed.

"Hey," she said, smiling. "I was wondering if you were going to make it inside before Christina started asking questions."

I let my bag thump to the floor and flopped backward onto my bed. "I just finished studying at the library. How was rehearsal?" I wanted to talk about anything but schoolwork. It was going to come up the second I started doing homework in a few minutes.

Khloe sat down, putting her script beside her. She looked cozy in a berry-colored cotton tee and matching plaid leggings. "Great," she said. "I nailed all of my lines! Maybe I was born to be a teapot. We worked on blocking, and guess what?"

"What?" I asked, smiling.

"Mr. Barber said we're *not* using old *Beauty and the Beast* costumes."

"Wow! That's awesome. I know you were worried about the old costume being too bulky. Have you seen the new ones?"

Khloe shook her head, almost bouncing on the bed.

"Nope! We're not buying them. *Your* fashion class is designing them and making them!"

That made me sit up. "We are?! Omigod! We're making actual clothes that people—you—are going to wear?"

Khloe had a Cheshire-Cat grin. "Yep! Mr. Barber said your fashion class teacher is making the announcement tomorrow with all of the details. I don't think you're making *all* of them, but you're definitely designing and sewing some."

"This is so cool! Ms. Snow told us to be thinking of a partner, and Cole and I already unofficially paired up. I'm so going to make sure we get to work on your costume."

"If you don't get mine, maybe you guys can get Riley's and be *creative*."

I pretended to write on my hand. Khloe had brought up Riley, so I had to tell her about the audition. Hopefully, Clare already had, but Khloe deserved to know if she hadn't. "Note taken. Speaking of You Know Who, did Clare tell you that we're going to be Riley free for a couple of days soon?"

Khloe pursed her lips. "No. What do you mean?"

"When I was studying tonight, Clare was at the library. She said that Riley sent in an audition tape to some casting director over the summer." The happy look on Khloe's face disappeared. "Apparently, the director wants to see her in person and she's going next weekend. But Riley hasn't told anybody because it's such a longshot. And you *know* if Riley's not telling people, she's not going to get it." I started talking faster, trying to stop Khloe's face from darkening by the second. "She's probably going to come back and make up a story that people in New York wanted to meet her and that she's up for a role or something. But she'll never hear back."

Khloe took in a big breath. "Whatever the deal, Riley's going to the city. Someone wants to see her for *something*."

"Khlo, I'm sorry. I didn't want to tell you because it's *no* big deal, but I also didn't want you to hear it somewhere else. If Riley's going to New York, she's splitting her rehearsal time between that and the play. Think about how hard you're working as Mrs. Potts and how she's spending less time on the play."

Now was *definitely* not the time to tell Khloe that her suspicions about Riley were wrong. It would only make her angrier toward the other girl.

Khloe shrugged and drew her legs up to her chest, wrapping her arms around them. "I'm working on a school play. Riley's practicing for a New York City audition. She's smart—she'll be an okay Belle and knock out her audition."

"But *you'll* be amazing," I argued. "People are going to

see this play. Important people. You're going to get the attention you deserve while Riley's distracted with something she's not going to get."

Khloe looked down at her hands, then back at me with a small smile. "Have I told you that you're a really good friend?"

"Nope," I said. "Never heard that from you before."

We smiled at each other.

"Maybe you're right," Khloe said. "I can't do anything about Riley's NYC audition. I'm jealous, sure, but it was wrong to knock the play. Everyone is working hard on it, and I'm proud of my role. I'm going to work even harder."

"That's my Khloe Kinsella."

Khloe and I chatted while I changed into pj's and set up my books at my desk. Khloe accepted my explanation that I hadn't finished all of my homework at the library because I'd gotten sidetracked. Khloe got into bed to read her lines and was asleep with the script on her chest hours before I turned off the desk light. I had a headache between my eyes, and without turning on a light, I tiptoed into the bathroom and took two Tylenol.

When I climbed into bed, I rubbed my forehead, realizing that it was time to do the one thing I'd been resisting until now. Tomorrow, I'd take care of it.

20

DECISION MADE

MS. UTZ FOLDED HER HANDS, STARING AT ME across her desk. "It's nice to see you, Lauren. What brought you to my office today?"

I was quiet for a second. I'd left lunch early, telling Khloe and Lexa that I had to meet one of my teachers. It was true—Ms. Utz taught my math class—but I wasn't coming to see her about math.

"I've been thinking a lot about my class schedule," I said. "I think I took on too much. I really, *really* don't want to ask, but am I able to change a class?"

"Lauren, of course," Ms. Utz said. She kept her eyes on me. "I'm glad you came to me about this. No matter how much I advised you to ease up your schedule, it had to be your decision. I'm here for guidance, not to force you to take one class or the other."

I scrunched my toes in my red ballet flats. "I kept telling myself that I'd figure out how to do everything and it would take time. But I realized I *do* have too many tough classes right now."

Ms. Utz turned to her computer, clicking her mouse. "You have several advanced courses, Lauren. I think if you were to make a change, you might find yourself able to excel even more. You wouldn't be stretched so thin and could give each class more attention to achieve the grades you desire."

"That's what I was hoping," I said, relaxing a little in the oversize leather chair. "I thought about the class that takes me the most time. I *love* Mr. Spellman's advanced history course, but it's incredibly time-consuming. Can I keep taking the same class but stop doing the advanced work to get regular credit?"

Ms. Utz looked back at her computer monitor and clicked a few more times. "Let's see . . ." I waited, crossing my fingers. "Yes," she said, finally. "I put a request through to Mr. Spellman. Unless you hear otherwise from me, please do not complete any of the assignments for advanced credit."

Très parfait!

"Thank you, Ms. Utz," I said.

"You're welcome," she said. "If you find that you're still struggling after this adjustment, I want you to set up another appointment with me. You're still taking a tough history course and, if necessary, we can transfer you to another class."

I promised her that I would keep her in the loop of how things worked out and left her office.

Lauren:

Good news 2 share w u ltr!

I sent the message to Khloe. My phone buzzed seconds later.

Oooh la la! ☺ Can't wait 2 hear! Learn something fun in French 2 teach me!

I pocketed my phone, feeling lighter with every step that I took toward Mme. Lafleur's classroom.

Later that afternoon, I was steps away from Ms. Snow's fashion class when my BlackBerry buzzed.

Drew:

How's ur day, L?

I stopped—midstep—and stared at my phone.

"Hey!" someone said, bumping into my arm. A dark-haired girl with green eyes shot me a look. "Don't just stop in the middle of the hallway. Are you trying to get run over?"

"Sorry," I said. Before I could apologize again, she was gone. I hurried over to the wall and flattened myself against it. I read Drew's message again.

Lauren:

Good! Fashion is nxt. Looking fwd 2 riding. U?

He wrote back immediately.

Drew:

☺ Glad ur having a good day. Same here. Catch u @ the stable?

Lauren:

Def. ☺ We could warm up 2gether if u want.

Drew:

4 sure. C u there.

I exited BBM and dashed through the doors of fashion class. Cole was already inside and in his usual seat. I took mine next to him, not even putting down my stuff before I grabbed his arm. Ms. Snow wasn't here yet, so I had a few precious seconds to talk to Cole.

"Cooooole!"

He looked at me sideways, laughing. "Laaaaaureeeen," he said, mimicking me. "What's up?"

"Drew BBMed me! Just now. Like, two seconds ago. He asked me how my day was. I said good. I asked him, and he said his was fine too. Then we said we'd warm up Whisper and Polo together."

I took a breath, needing one after the mouthful I'd just spit out at Cole.

"Whoa, LT." Cole grinned. "Sounds like you made the right decision about Drew, huh?"

I nodded. "Thanks to you. I saw Ms. Utz today and got approval to switch from advanced history to regular credit. It's going to make everything *so* much more manageable."

Cole offered me a palm for a high-five. "That's great! You did this all on your own. I'm sure the change will make a huge difference in everything."

We fell silent when Ms. Snow entered the classroom.

"Good afternoon, everyone," Ms. Snow said. My eyes went to her outfit—she definitely won the Best Dressed Teacher award. Today, she'd paired tall black boots with flared black pants and a red silk shirt with adorable gold buttons down the front.

"I want to start class by discussing the elusive project that I've mentioned a couple times," she said. "I've told you to get to know someone else in class—someone you feel compatible to work with. That will be vital today because you will each be signing up with a partner for our first class project."

Hands went into the air. "What is it?" asked Allie, a girl with red-framed glasses.

Ms. Snow smiled. "I've been working with the theater department and have been in discussion with Mr. Barber, the drama coach, about the fall production of *Beauty and the Beast*."

Everyone exchanged glances.

"Our class is being given a wonderful opportunity to be hands-on with the play this season," Ms. Snow continued. "We are going to redesign and create many of the costumes for the seventh grade production."

"What?"

"Omigod!"

"We are?!"

Everyone started talking at once.

"No way!" Cole said. He looked at me, eyes wide. "Did you know about this?"

I smiled. "Khloe told me yesterday. We *have* to get her costume!"

Ms. Snow, smiling, let us talk and get it out of our systems. I listened to murmurs of "I have no clue how to sew!" to "I'm sketching Belle's costume in my head already. Who plays her? It's that girl Riley, right?"

"All right, everyone," Ms. Snow said, putting up her

hands in a quiet-it-down motion. "Let me explain how this will work. I'm going to pass around a sign-up sheet. Write down your name and your partner's. This evening, I'll look over the selections and will assign each pairing a costume at random. There's no reason for worry—I will not be expecting you to begin sketching and creating a costume immediately. We will have several classes before we even begin discussing how to create a new costume."

Today was *très* amazing! One more class after fashion, then I'd be at the stable. With Drew. And tonight I'd be able to actually hang out with Khloe because I wouldn't have to stay up past lights-out to finish homework. She was going to be so happy. When the sign-up sheet reached me, I signed my name next to Cole's with a flourish.

That night, Khloe was stretched out on her bed, having finished her homework about an hour ago, and was reading the latest *Entertainment Weekly*. She'd asked a zillion times what "good news" I had, but I'd ducked her questions, wanting to surprise her. I'd changed the topic to my warm-up session with Drew, which had been the perfect distraction. Khloe had asked a dozen questions, and I'd been only too happy to spill every detail. Drew and I had ridden together and I'd felt what I'd always thought was impossible—that clichéd electricity in the air between us.

Now I closed my books, packed them up, and swiveled in my desk chair to look at her.

"Want to watch a movie?" I asked.

Khloe looked up, one eyebrow arched. "What?"

"Movie? There's a new comedy that looks good."

Khloe slowly put down her magazine. "How can we watch a movie," she started. "You have a ton of home-work, don't you?"

I got up and plopped on my bed, grinning at her. "Nope! I'm done!"

Khloe shook her head. "Did you work during a class or something?"

"Even better. I left lunch early to go see Ms. Utz. Khlo, you and Lex were right. I needed to lighten my schedule."

Khloe's brown eyes brightened. "Omigod! Laur! Really?!"

"Really," I confirmed. "I know I fought you before. I was really embarrassed and I wanted to do everything I said I would. But zero free time wasn't fun. I wanted to hang out with you after riding and not be chained to my desk."

"What did you change in your schedule?" Khloe asked. She sat up, straightening her white pocket tee that went with blue-and-gray striped leggings.

"History," I said. "Mr. Spellman's class takes too much time. I switched from advanced to regular credit. If there's a problem with it, and Ms. Utz doesn't think there will be, I'll transfer into a different class."

Khloe looked down, picking at her bedspread. "You might change history classes?"

"Probably not," I said. "I don't want to. I think Mr. S will be cool with everything and I'll keep the same schedule."

"Did Ms. Utz suggest history or did you?" Khloe's tone had lost its earlier excitement. I didn't understand why she was fixated on history.

"I did," I said. "Khlo, I thought you'd be happy about this. What's wrong?"

Khloe shook her head. "Nothing. I'm happy, really, that you're going to have free time. You deserve it. I just . . ."

"What?" I asked, my tone soft.

"History is the only class we have by ourselves. I hope you don't get transferred."

I sat back a little. She didn't think—I mean—there was no way she thought I'd tried to switch classes *because* of her. "Khloe, I won't get transferred. You *know* I picked history because of the workload. I definitely do *not* want to be yanked from a class we have together."

Khloe gave me a tiny nod. "I know. Sorry I acted weird. I'm *really*, really happy that you saw Ms. Utz. Having more time to hang out is awesome." She smiled. "You pick a movie and I'll go make popcorn. Depending on what movie we choose, maybe it'll give us ideas for Riley payback."

And it was definitely time to tell her before she concocted a full plan.

"Khlo, the other night when I was at the library, I asked Jill about the DVD," I said. "I asked if there was any way that Riley could have planted it somehow."

Khloe's eyes widened. "Omigod! I totally wasn't planning to ask anyone—I was thinking a rogue mission—but what did Jill say?"

"Unfortunately, and I mean *very* unfortunately," I said, "Jill swore that Riley had zero alone time with the DVDs. Jill said she handpicked the DVD and there was no way Riley had tagged it somehow for her to choose. It really was an accident."

Khloe started to shake her head. "Maybe Riley sneaked out in the middle of the night . . ."

"And assumed we'd watch a horse show in the morning?" I smiled sympathetically. "I'm sorry, but it wasn't Riley. Not this time."

Khloe sighed. "Well, I *guess* there's still time."

"Time until we graduate," I said, smiling.

That made Khloe smile back. "So, Riley is innocent *this* time. But she'll slip up and we'll be ready!"

Khloe hopped off her bed and was out the door before I could reply. I sat alone in our room, second-guessing my decision about visiting Ms. Utz. It felt like I'd been doing a lot of that lately.

21

GUESS WHO'S NOT
ON THE LIST?

"IT'S OUT! THE LIST IS OUT!" KHLOE POUNCED onto the end of my bed as I blinked, still half asleep. The glowing numbers on my clock revealed 6:57 on Friday morning.

"You *never* get up before me," I said. "What's out?"

Khloe looked at me like I'd asked her what year it was. "The *list*! I already printed it, but I haven't read it yet."

"Ohh! I forgot about that. My first official list," I said. "Let's look."

I rubbed my eyes and Khloe crawled next to me, tossing my comforter over her legs and leaning back against my pillows that I'd fluffed up. She seemed like normal Khloe—not the Khloe I'd seen a flash of last night—though it wasn't like her to be awake this early. Or, awake this early *willingly*.

Khloe and I each held a corner of the paper like it was some kind of ancient scroll.

"Ahh! Jill made Most Likely to be Class President!" Khloe said. "She's going to love that."

"And look, Clare's Potential Girl Next Door! Whoa," I said. "That's cool."

"Omigod, she must be *freaking* out."

Khloe and I kept scanning the list, reading different names and awards to each other.

"Look, look," Khloe said. "Drew's Most Likely to Be Swim Team Captain."

"That will make him so happy. Or it will if he cares about the list," I said.

I reached for my phone, wanting to text him the news. Maybe he'd think it was silly, but I thought it was cool. Making captain was a big deal and *someone* at Canterwood thought he had the potential. Not a teacher, but someone close to his age. That made it a bigger deal.

"Oooh, Khloeeee," I said. "Zack's on the list too!"

Khloe looked over at the paper. "Most Likely MVP," she said, grinning. "Um, *yeah!*"

I giggled. "Does it mean Most Valuable Player, like sports, or Most Valuable *Player*?"

Khloe squinted, tapping her forehead. "I'm going to go with sports. Just because, you know, I don't want him to be a player!"

"It better be about sports if he's dating *my* roommate," I said.

But Khloe was staring at the piece of paper as if she hadn't even heard me.

"Khlo?"

"You made the list!" Khloe said, looking up to meet my gaze. "Lauren!"

"I did?! Where?" I looked where Khloe had planted her finger, her nail painted Essie Raspberry.

"My roomie is on the list! You got Most Potential to Be Popular!" Khloe pushed her shoulder into mine. "This is huge! I mean, I already knew you were popular, but you're on the radar."

"This is so weird. I haven't done anything to be 'popular,'" I said. "But I'll take it. It *is* kind of cool."

Khloe had her phone out, texting. "I'm telling Lexa and Clare. Today is the best day ever! You made the list *and* I have a date tonight!"

We laughed. I picked up my phone again to finish my BBM to Drew.

Lauren:

R the guys in Blackwell going crazy like Hawthorne girls right now? Have u seen The List?

Drew is typing a message.

I watched my phone. "He's writing back," I said. "I just wrote him."

"Someone's taking his phone everywhere," Khloe teased in a singsong voice.

Drew:

Don't tell, but guys just as into it as the girls. ☺ *I just saw ur name, Miss Popular! Congrats.*

Lauren:

shakes head Pls don't call me that, lol! & what abt U?? *salutes captain*

Drew:

Oh, geez. LOL. Thanks. U should come c me swim some time.

Lauren:

I'd like that. ☺

Drew:

Gotta get ready, but TTYL!

Lauren:

Bye!

I exited BBM, grinning.

"Drew just asked me to watch him swim," I said. "Oh my God."

"That," Khloe said, "is awesome." She looked back at her phone screen.

"Um, Khloe?"

"What?" She looked up from her BlackBerry.

"There was a name we missed. You're on the list." I bit my bottom lip, looking at her with wide eyes. "I'm sorry, K. I feel like I need to be the one to show you. You shouldn't be alone when you see this."

Khloe put down her phone. She looked at me. "Just tell me. I guess nasty categories started this year."

I took a deep breath. "Khloe, you were named . . . Most Likely Broadway Star!"

I burst into laughter, shoving the paper in front of her. "Sorry, but I had to, after all the times you've gotten me. Look!"

"No way. No way!" Khloe's finger hovered below the words.

Khloe Kinsella: Most Likely Broadway Star.

"Khloeee!" I twisted around to hug her. "You *so* deserve that! *Oh, mon Dieu!*"

Khloe shook her head, looking dazed. "I can't believe

it. It's like it's a joke and my name's going to disappear."

"It's no joke. You, my dear roommate and best friend, are on your way to discovery. I'm so proud!"

I slid off the bed, walking across the room and opening our door.

"What are you doing?" Khloe asked.

"Making sure everyone knows!" I said.

I took the purple dry-erase marker from the ledge on our door's whiteboard and erased *Khloe & Lauren are out!* with my hand. In its place I wrote *Khloe Kinsella: Voted Most Likely Broadway Star!!* I drew a star and wrote, *She lives HERE!*

Khloe's brown eyes got teary. "Laur, geez. You're so sweet."

"I *told* you that all of the hard work you're doing was going to pay off. Do you see a name missing from this list?"

"Riley's." Khloe didn't even pause.

"Exactly. Let her go to New York on a chance. This list is certain, and you're on it."

"This is like a daytime talk-show fest, but I'm hugging you again!" Khloe said, grabbing me. Together, we got ready for class, talking about the list and everything we were going to do this afternoon to prep Khloe for her date. When we were ready, Khloe and I linked arms and left Hawthorne.

22

TU ET MOI—DÉJEUNER?

FRIDAY CLASSES FLEW BY. TEACHERS WERE
oddly nice about weekend homework and barely assigned
any. Plus, it was as if the goodwill flowed to the stable.
An e-mail had been in my inbox this morning from Mr.
Conner. He'd given the seventh-grade intermediate and
advanced teams the afternoon off from practice. An afternoon off from lessons sounded so good and the timing
was even better. Khloe had freaked that we would have
more time to prep for date night. My phone buzzed in the
middle of Mr. Davidson's English class. We were all reading to ourselves, so I pulled my phone out of my pocket
and hid it behind the pages of my textbook.

Drew:

Hey! U wanna grab lunch @ SS?

I read and reread the message. Then I translated it to French. *Tu et moi—déjeuner?* I typed to Khloe, who was sitting next to me.

Lauren:

!! Drew just asked me 2 lunch @ SS!!

Khloe's head popped up and she grinned at me. She held her phone low and typed.

Khloe:

Today is AWESOME! Go! Write him now and say yes!

Lauren:

I'm going 2! OMG! ☺

I exited my chat with Khloe and opened Drew's convo.

Lauren:

Hi! That would b great! Meet u there in 45 mins?

Drew:

Cool ☺ *C u soon.*

"All right," Mr. Davidson said. "You should have finished the section on memoirs. Let's discuss."

I hurried to scan the last half page.

"Khloe," Mr. Davidson said. "What would make you pick up a memoir?"

Khloe looked at our teacher. "The topic. If I related to the author, I'd want to read it. Or, if it was interesting, I'd probably read it."

Mr. Davidson moved around the room asking questions. Luckily, he didn't call on me. If he had, I probably would have said, "*The Autobiography of Drew Adams* sounds good."

"Text me after!" Khloe said. We stood outside the English building with Clare, who'd walked out with us after class.

"I will," I said. "Do I look okay?" When I'd gotten dressed this morning, I hadn't planned on meeting Drew for lunch.

"You look great," Khloe said. "Perfect for a lunch date."

"Yeah," Clare said. "Effortlessly chic."

"Thanks, guys," I said. My messenger bag was on the ground, and I was checking lip gloss with a compact mirror and finger-combing my waves. I dropped my mirror into my bag and smoothed my Calvin Klein heather-gray three-quarter-sleeve shirt, ran my hands over the tops of my black skinny jeans, and made sure my ebony leather ballet flats with tiny bows were dirt free.

"Go," Khloe said. "You'll have a great time."

With one last smile at her and Clare, I turned in the opposite direction of the cafeteria and started for The Sweet Shoppe. The high September sun warmed my skin and I squinted to see. Other students with the same lunch time or free period had the same idea as Drew. They headed in the direction of The Slice or The Sweet Shoppe, or picnicked on the grass. Under a shady maple tree, two blond girls—one with darker, long blond hair and the other with a platinum chin-length bob—had spread a giant purple blanket and sipped Diet Coke and chatted.

I focused on the students, trying not to get inside my head about lunch with Drew. I could do this. I'd *done* this. It was just lunch with a guy. I'd dated Taylor for five months, but this felt different somehow. I really wanted this to go well. Drew was cute, funny, *and* a rider.

A week ago, I would have texted Ana, Brielle, or Becca. I would have told them how nervous I was about meeting Drew, how I wasn't sure if it was the right thing to do, and how I wasn't sure if it was too soon after Taylor.

Today, as I reached the steps of The Sweet Shoppe, I didn't need to ask anyone for their opinion. I wanted to trust my gut—New Lauren did that. It didn't mean I wasn't going to go to my friends, but it did make me feel stronger. Becca would be proud.

I walked inside The Sweet Shoppe, my mood lifting instantly from the delicious smells. The store was less crowded than usual since most students were at lunch or in class. I shifted my bag and glanced around the room, stepping away from the line and toward the clusters of tables.

Immediately, I spotted Drew. He wasn't hard to miss. His black hair, medium length and slightly curly, was shocking against his skin. He raised a hand, smiling. I started toward him, weaving around tables and people, not seeing anything but his sapphire-blue eyes.

"Hi," I said, reaching him.

"Hey, Laur," Drew said. "That looks heavy." He reached over and lifted my bag from my shoulder, taking it from me. "Is this table okay? We can move if you want."

"It's perfect," I said. Drew had chosen a cute square table. The white table had two matching chairs—white with sky-blue polka dots.

"Cool," Drew said. He pulled out a chair, motioning for me to sit.

"Thanks," I said. I loved that Drew was one of *those* boys. He pulled out his date's chair. Definitely something to tell Becs when we talked.

Drew sat across from me, putting my bag next to his black backpack.

"I'm glad you were free," Drew said. "I see you with Lexa and Khloe a lot. You guys seem close."

"We are," I said, smiling. "Khloe is . . ." I laughed. "Khloe's unlike *anyone* I've ever met. She's become my best friend. You won't want to hear the long story of what she did when we first met, but I will say it's never boring to have an actress as a roommate."

"I like long stories," Drew said. "What if I get us something to eat and you tell me over lunch?"

I had a crazy hot and cold flash all at once. "That sounds great," I managed to get out. "You better order lots of food for yourself. Don't say I didn't warn you that it was a long story."

Winking, Drew picked up the menu and slid it between us. "I'll order two of everything to be safe." He took my order and headed up to the counter.

This was *très parfait*! I couldn't fight liking Drew if I tried. I peeked over my shoulder, and Drew was still a couple of people away from the counter. I leaned down and grabbed my phone from my bag.

Lauren:

UM, we haven't even started talking or eating, but he is SO CUTE!

A BBM came back seconds later.

Khloe:

!! ☺ Ahhh! I knew it would b amaze!

Lauren:

He pulled out my *chair.* Who does that anymore??

Khloe:

No 1 except 4 nice guys like Drew.

Lauren:

GTG but OMG! ☺ Can't wait 2 tell u abt it ltr.

Khloe:

Lex is w me & she said 2 tell u she's freaking out. ☺ TTYL!

I put my phone away before Drew came back. He stopped in front of our table, balancing trays. I took the cardboard holder with two of The Sweet Shoppe's signature hot-beverage cups and plastic lids. Drew put down everything else.

"Thank you so much," I said.

"No problem," Drew said. He sat, pushing a huge tray between us.

I giggled, looking at the tray's size. "You took my advice, huh? Did you leave food for anyone else?"

Drew feigned innocence. "I have *no* idea what you're talking about."

"Hmmm." I looked at the tray. "Let's see: three cupcakes—vanilla, chocolate, and strawberry—slices of cherry and apple pie, an assortment of cookies, and—" I stopped. "Petits fours." I met Drew's eyes. Five dark-chocolate petits fours were drizzled with light-blue chocolate.

"I can take those back if you don't want them," Drew said.

"Are you kidding? I love those!" I looked at him, realizing he was teasing. "They're amazing. I'm taking French *and* that's my favorite shade of blue—it's like you knew."

"I *did* know about French, but blue *might* have come up in casual conversation with Khloe."

"When did you guys talk?" I asked. "She's such a sneak—she didn't even tell me. I picked up my cup of white pear tea. I took a cautious sip, not wanting to burn my tongue.

"We have our ways," Drew said, taking a bite of apple pie. He gave me an *I'm so mysterious* look.

"Oh, yeah?" I asked.

"Okay, okay, so our 'ways' are running into each other in the tack room. I asked Khloe what you liked and made her swear not to tell you. Don't get mad at her for breaking girl code or something."

I smiled. "I'm not mad. I would have done the same for her. This"—I gestured to our table—"is so thoughtful. No one's done anything like this for me in a long time."

"I'm really glad you like it," Drew said.

We reached for different desserts and a million questions for him ran through my head.

"I know you swim," I said. "I haven't been to the Canterwood pool yet."

"You definitely have to come. Sometime, when we're not having practice, we could swim laps together or something. It's the best."

"What made you love swimming?"

Drew took a sip of his lemonade. "Before I joined any swim teams, I used to go to my uncle's every summer. He lives in this part of rural Tennessee with a lake and dock. He taught me how to swim. After a couple of summers, I asked my dad if I could join a swim team. We found one at the YMCA and I swam there until I came to Canterwood."

"That's so cool. I've never been to Tennessee," I said. "Or really out in the country like that either."

"My uncle Dan lives *really* out there—like, gravel roads and everything." Drew grinned. "He let me drive his truck last year."

"Lucky! My parents won't even let me sit in the driver's seat," I said.

"Don't be too jealous. I drove his trunk around a giant

field with nothing but rolls of hay. I haven't been within miles of a road."

We laughed. Drew had one of the best laughs. It was something I paid attention to in people I met. His was deep, and when he really got laughing, his eyes seemed to turn an even more brilliant blue.

"I have a pool," I said. "I love swimming, but swimming in a lake sounds scary."

"You've never done it?"

"Nope." I shook my head. "It would have to be crystal-clear water with a view of the bottom. The thought of swimming and a fish or something brushing against me creeps me out."

"I bet I could get you in a lake if you were with me," Drew said. "I wouldn't let anything—not even a minnow—near you."

I tilted my head. "I'll have to think about that. Maybe if you convinced your uncle to let me drive."

Drew laughed. "I'll see what I can do."

I bit into a delicious vanilla cupcake.

"So, you know I've made it out alive from swimming in a lake. What's your history with riding?"

"Well, um, you know I rode competitively. I started really young and traveled a lot. It was my whole life, and after my accident, I needed a break."

Drew shook his head. "I can't imagine what you went through. I'm sorry."

"Thanks," I said. "But it got me to Canterwood. If I'd kept competing, I probably would have lost sight of why I started riding in the first place—because I *love* horses. Taking a break gave me time to think. I realized coming here was what I wanted."

"To compete?" Drew asked.

"Yes, but not like before. I'm never putting a ribbon before a horse or myself again. I want to enjoy riding *and* showing."

"How're you feeling about the schooling show?"

I licked icing off my cupcake. "About as many emotions as my brain can handle! I'm scared, excited, thinking about my past shows, proud to show off Whisper—a mess of things."

Drew shifted in his seat. "I don't think it would be normal if you weren't a little nervous. But I bet showing your own horse will help."

"I think so too. We're really connected, and I don't think I'll feel alone in the arena."

"We should practice together," Drew said, picking up his drink. "Polo needs work and so do I. Interested?"

"Definitely." I smiled. "That would be great."

We sipped our drinks and talked horses for a few more minutes. Awkward pauses never happened, and it was as if we were friends who had a lot of catching up to do.

"Where are you from?" I asked.

"Hartford," Drew said. "It's less than twenty minutes from here. I live with my dad. My parents split a few years ago and Mom lives in Seattle."

I saw something—maybe pain—flicker in his eyes when he brought up his mom.

"I'm sorry," I said. "That must be hard. Do you see your mom a lot?"'

Drew shook his head. "Not really. I've been to her place once, and she comes a couple of times a year to see me, but we're not close. My dad's the best, though." He smiled. "What about you?"

"Union's home," I said. "I moved a lot, but I think my family's settled in Union now. My mom's a lawyer and Dad's a writer. I've got two older sisters—Charlotte and Becca."

Drew asked me more questions about my family, and I told him about my relationships with Becca and Char. We talked and kept talking—my tea was gone long ago and we'd eaten every bit of food that Drew had ordered. We'd even picked up stray sprinkles.

At the same time, our heads swiveled to the wall clock, as if instinct had kicked in.

"Uh-oh," Drew said.

"The clock *has* to be wrong," I said. "It's not—"

"We missed our next class," Drew said. "I'm sorry, Lauren. I should have paid attention. I don't want you to get in trouble. I'll tell your teacher something—that I made you late."

"It's not your fault," I said. "We were both talking and not watching the clock."

I waited for the impulse to jump up and start clearing the table. But I didn't move. And neither did he. The guiltiness I waited for—the chastising myself for missing class—didn't come.

"Talking to you caused me to accidentally ditch class for the first time," I said, smiling. "Ever."

Drew shook his head. "Great first impression. What class?"

I laughed. "French, ironically. But you *did* get me petits fours, so I think that should count for something."

"I had fun," Drew said.

"Me too. Thanks for asking me."

"Maybe we can do this again?" Drew smiled. "I promise not to make you late next time."

"Hmmm . . ." I rolled my eyes to the ceiling, pretending to think. "I *guess* that sounds good." I grinned. "The not-being-late part really sealed my decision."

We laughed and, together, started clearing the table. I'd find Mme. Lafleur later and apologize and offer to do extra credit or whatever necessary to keep up my grade. That didn't mean I regretted my decision. I would miss French all over again for the *très parfait* lunch with Drew.

23

ROOMMATE
GONE BAD

"DREW TOTALLY CORRUPTED YOU! MY GOOD roommate has gone bad!" Khloe said, giggling.

I laughed. "I'm cutting class every week now." I swished my toes in the plastic tub that held my soaking feet. After our last classes, Khloe and I had turned our room into a spa. I'd told Khloe to feel free to take an extra-long hot shower, telling her I'd use it tonight while she was out. Now Khloe's wet hair was wrapped in a towel and we were in terry-cloth robes.

"This is *so* perfect," Khloe said, sighing. "I get to gossip with my roomie *and* get pretty for Zack all at the same time."

"It's only the first station," I said. "We've got nails, face, hair, and makeup left."

I inhaled, loving the scents of lavender, rose, and mint. We were both at our desk chairs, feet in basins filled with warm water and rose-scented foot-softening gel.

"I think I'm ready to scrub now," I said, lifting a foot out of the water.

"Me too," Khloe said.

Both of us had dug out our mani-pedi kits. I reached into mine and pulled out my pumice stone. I rubbed it over my left foot until the skin was smooth. Khloe did the same, and we dried our feet, then slathered them with minty lotion. We pulled on fuzzy socks to seal in the moisture.

"The warmth from your body heat and the socks seals in the moisture," Khloe said. "EBT."

"Good one. Mani time!" I said. "I'll do your nails, Khlo."

Khloe smiled. "Yay! Thanks, LT. I'm not the best polisher ever."

"No problem. No way were you doing your own nails today—date or no date. Let me set up my salon."

I filled a small dish with water and poured in gel that turned the water a light pink. I put that bowl, a hand towel, and my nail kit on a spare clipboard on a lap tray on my bed. Our nail polish collection was out, and Khloe was going through the colors.

"Come on over when you've got one," I said.

Khloe held up two bottles of OPI. "I'm torn," she said. "Am I feeling bold and red à la Keys to My Karma or girly and Elephantastic Pink?"

"Both are great colors. I think you're more of a bold girl. Go red."

Khloe nodded. "You're so right. I think I'll do my toes pink or purple."

"Love," I said. "I'll probably do my nails some shade of pink. I don't know about my toes yet."

Khloe sat cross-legged on my bed and put one hand into the dish. I took her other hand and held up the nail file.

"Square or round, miss?" I asked.

"Square, please. Thank you."

I giggled, starting to file. "This is fun. We have to do spa days more often."

Khloe nodded. "For sure. We deserve it to de-stress."

"This length okay?" I motioned to Khloe's right hand.

"Perfect. I think you're on your way to a *big* tip."

I laughed and switched the water dish to the other side, so Khloe's freshly smoothed nails could soak. I filed the nails on her other hand, then started the rest of the mani process. Khloe leaned back, eyes flickering shut, as

I pushed back her cuticles, scrubbed her hands with an apricot-smelling exfoliant, rubbed on lotion, swiped polish remover over her nails, buffed them, and painted on a base coat.

"My hands feel *so* good," Khloe said. "Thank you so much, Laur."

"Of course," I said, smiling. "Zack's probably—*no*, definitely—going to hold your hand. When he does, it's *got* to be ultra-soft."

I picked up the red OPI polish, rolling the bottle between my palms. That was an EBT I'd taught Khloe.

"I can't even think about that," Khloe said. "I'm so nervous!"

"It's going to be so much fun that you'll forget about being nervous," I said. "Tell me the date plan again. And keep your hands still while I paint."

Khloe took a deep breath. "Okay. Still. I can be still. Oh, date plan."

I leaned over, painting a streak of red onto her nail. I'd never seen Khloe so flustered. She was always the outgoing, ready-for-anything girl. But tonight's date made her adorably nervous. She'd even shampooed her hair twice by accident.

"Zack's meeting me in front of Christina's office

at seven," Khloe said. "We're going to The Slice first. I already thought about the menu and know what I'm getting."

"What?"

"Caesar salad and some kind of pizza. I'm *not* getting anything messy or weird to eat in front of Zack. Like spaghetti. That would be so embarrassing to eat!"

I nodded, painting her ring finger. "It's definitely cuter in *Lady and the Tramp* when the dogs push the meatballs around with their noses and share a spaghetti strand."

"Exactly! So after we eat, I'll excuse myself and hit the bathroom. I packed my purse with everything I need."

I looked up at her. "Everything . . . ? Like what?"

"Like, a mirror in case the one in the bathroom is gone or broken."

"Oh, right. Because giant mirrors *do* go missing all of the time." I grinned. "I should remember that."

"Lauren!" Khloe wailed, sticking out her bottom lip. "I'm serious! You have to listen to my list and help me in case I've forgotten something. You can tease me *after* my date."

"You're totally right. Listening." I started painting her opposite hand. I realized Khloe was half-kidding and half-serious. Maybe she needed to be overprepared so she wouldn't be so nervous. If that were true, I understood. "Okay, so you've got a mirror. What else?"

"Powder. Girls on dates always excuse themselves to 'powder their noses' or something. I'll do that. Then I'll use a travel-size toothbrush and tiny toothpaste and brush my teeth."

I nodded slowly. "Okay. That's not a bad idea."

"I'm not sure if I want us to kiss on the first date, but what if I want to and we do?" Khloe asked. Her voice was unusually high and she talked faster than normal. "I want to smell like mint. Minty fresh is how my breath should smell. Do you think I should take mouthwash? I don't have any travel-size ones. My bottle of Scope won't fit in my purse and—"

"Khloe," I said softly. I put down the polish and grasped her upper arms gently. "You don't need mouthwash. As your bestie and roomie, I'm not letting you leave with a giant bottle of germ-fighting liquid poking out of your purse. You don't want to look like you tried too hard, you know?" Khloe nodded, taking another breath. "Brushing your teeth will be plenty, I promise. Did you pack more?"

I picked up the polish for a second coat.

"Not too much. Just a Tide stick in case I spill something, two extra lip glosses if I lose one or don't want to smell like bubble gum or cotton candy, a phone charger in case my battery dies and I need to text you for advice, sticky notes with questions to ask Zack, a pack of Kleenex if I get a runny nose, cough drops, and a mini hairbrush." Khloe closed her eyes for a second. "Yep, that's everything."

I painted the second coat of red onto her last nail, nodding. "You're definitely very prepared. After dinner, you're going to the movies, right?"

Khloe nodded. "We didn't decide on what movie. Should I pick? Or let him? What if I choose something he doesn't like?"

"Decide together. There are a ton of movies out right now that look good."

"Together, okay," Khloe said, almost as if she was trying to memorize my suggestion.

I painted a thin coat of Essie's No Chips Ahead top coat onto Khloe's nails so they were glossy in the light. "Look," I said. "You have awesome nails!"

Khloe held up a hand. "Oh, wow! I got so distracted—I almost forgot you were doing them. I'm sorry, Laur. Thank you—you did an amazing job!"

"Don't apologize, and you're welcome." I got up and brought back the polish bin for Khloe to choose a color for her toes. "You're going to do great, Khloe. Really. If Zack doesn't have fun with you, it's his loss. You're the coolest girl I know."

Khloe gave me a wobbly smile. "And you're the sweetest roommate. You're helping me feel so much better."

"And making your nails so much prettier!" I said. "Let's talk toenail polish."

I kept Khloe distracted while I did her toes with the royal purple she'd chosen. After I'd finished, we slathered our faces with Freeman's avocado mask. I'd do my nails later.

"We look like the witch from *Wicked*," Khloe said, giggling at our green faces. We let the masks dry, washed them off with warm water, and then Khloe dried her hair. While she straightened her shiny blond locks with the flat iron, I checked my phone. I had a couple of unread BBMs.

Drew:

Had fun 2day. Did u get in trouble w French teacher? I told my math teacher I got sick after lunch & he believed me. I'm such a bad liar, tho! Whew.

Brielle:

Hey, LT! So srry I haven't written u back in 4ever. School's been crazy. Nothing new here. Catch up soon! Love u! xx

I responded to Drew first.

Lauren:

*Had fun 2! Glad u didn't get in trouble. Me either. Told Mme.
Lafleur the same. We're not serial skippers, so I think 1x is OK.* ☺

Then Brielle.

*Totes understand! Maybe we can Skype this wkend? I miss ur
face, LOL. Love u 2!*

I put down my phone just as Khloe unplugged the flat
iron. "Did I miss any spots?" she asked, turning so I could
see the back of her head.

"Nope, your hair looks great," I said. "I never get mine
that straight."

Khloe checked her phone. "Omigod, he's going to be
here in an hour. An hour!"

"Plenty of time for clothes and makeup. We've got
this!"

I pulled open Khloe's closet door, motioning like a
saleswoman to her outfits. "What're you thinking?"

Khloe padded over in her slippers. "I want to look
casual, but kind of dressy. Ideas? You have the best outfits."

I smiled. "Thanks, KK. I think you'd look amazing
in . . ." I stepped up to her closet, pulling out items and
arranging them on her bed. "Skinny black jeans, the silk
purple shirt *or* the clover-green capped-sleeve shirt, a black
cardigan in case it's chilly at the restaurant or the theater,

and ballet flats—style and color to be determined upon your choice of shirt."

"You're the best," Khloe said, playing with the ends of her terry-cloth robe belt. "I love the jeans and purple shirt."

"Yay! That's what I would have picked for you. The cut's flattering and I love the faux pearl buttons." I leaned down and picked up shoes from her closet floor. "These?"

Khloe smiled, looking totally relaxed for the first time all day. "Definitely yes!" I put the black peep-toe flats at the bottom of her bed.

"You're going to look amazing! The shoes will show off your toenail polish."

"It's such a relief to have an outfit picked out," Khloe said. "I knew you'd know what I should wear, but I was seriously stressing over it."

"Stress no more. It's *the* outfit. So, I was thinking about makeup and wondered if you wanted to do your own *or* if you wanted me to do it."

Khloe clasped her hands together, her red nails flashing in the light. "Would you? That would be so cool! But you totally don't have to either. You've done so much for me, and you haven't gotten to paint your nails yet or even shower."

"I offered! I'd really love to do your makeup."

Squealing, Khloe stepped over and hugged me. "Tell me where to sit."

I directed her to my desk chair, aka "makeup chair," and started with a dime-size amount of moisturizer. I kept everything simple and let Khloe's blemish-free, tan skin be as untouched as possible. I applied shimmery caramel eye shadow, a little concealer under her eyes, one coat of brown-black mascara, a dusting of peachy blush, and a shiny coat of Sephora Glossy Gloss in a rosy pink to her lips.

"Done," I said, handing her a mirror. "Like it?"

Khloe looked into the handheld mirror. "I love it! I look like *me* and not like I caked on five pounds of makeup."

Ten minutes later, Khloe was dressed and checking her reflection head to toe in our floor-length mirror.

"How do you feel?" I asked. "Because you look like you're ready for a date!"

Khloe turned, smiling at me. "Thanks to you, I feel awesome. I don't feel all sweaty and crazy-nervous anymore. You gave me the royal treatment today. I'm so paying you back—just wait."

"I'm so glad you feel good," I said. "But it's not a payback thing. You're my friend and I wanted to do something nice for you. I say you put on your glass slippers, Cinderella, and go meet Prince Zack."

"Ohmigoshomigosh!" Khloe said, making us both laugh. She put on her shoes, hugged me again, and grabbed her purse.

"This," Khloe said, reaching into her purse and pulling out a giant Ziploc bag, "is staying here." She tossed the bag onto her bed. "See you later."

"Good luck, and BBM me if you need anything!"

Khloe tossed me one last smile and slipped out the door. I looked at the bag she'd left behind—the brush, Tide stick, and everything she'd thought she needed—and put it in her closet. A good feeling settled over me as I got ready to shower. Khloe was going to be more than fine—she'd proved that the second she'd tossed her bag of "necessities."

24

TELL ME
ALL ABOUT IT

AFTER I GOT OUT OF THE SHOWER AND DRIED
my hair, I settled onto my bed with a pile of books. If
I could get some homework done now, it would give
me more free time to practice with Whisper before the
schooling show.

My heart seemed to pound an extra beat when I
thought about the show. I pictured riding Whisper in
front of judges for our classes. I saw us completing dressage moves and flowing in tandem. Then I imagined us
conquering obstacles for the trail-riding class. Maybe
opening and closing a gate or crossing a bridge. *You're going
to start practicing more tomorrow,* I reminded myself. *And Khloe
agreed to help.* I needed to stop making myself nervous.

I got up, wanting tea before I started homework. I

slid my feet into flip-flops and bypassed our microwave. Teakettle water was what I wanted. I walked down to the Hawthorne common room, stepping inside. Riley and Clare were under an oversize fleece throw on the couch watching a movie. Clare looked up, smiling. Riley did the same, but there was no warmth behind her smile.

I walked around the counter, glad to have it as a barrier between us, and filled the empty teakettle. I turned the flame on high and pulled down the box of tea with my name on it. Sifting through the teas, I tried to decide what I wanted. Definitely something of the white variety.

"Missed you in French class."

I jumped, almost dropping a packet of white tea on the floor. Riley moved like a ghost! "Yeah, I wasn't feeling well." I kept my gaze on the tea, pretending to be reading the name of every packet, hoping Riley would get the hint and go back to her movie.

"Aw, well, who *would* feel well after eating so much dessert at The Sweet Shoppe."

I looked up, my eyes meeting Riley's. "Is there a rule about dessert that I don't know about?"

"Of course not," Riley said, holding my gaze. "But there *is* one about attending class. I don't know *how* you did it—convincing Madame Lafleur to allow you to miss

French so you could hang out with Drew. You have to tell me your secret!"

I set my jaw, determined not to let Riley get to me. "If you're going to tell on me like we're in second grade, go ahead. I'm sure you have some way to prove I was at The Sweet Shoppe when I should have been in class."

"I never said that," Riley said. "I just asked how you managed to skip detention. That's really hard to do here. Impressive, really."

The water in the kettle started to boil. "Actually, it's not anything worth talking about since I'm not doing it again. I'm sure you can figure it out if you want."

Riley folded her arms. "Smart to keep it to yourself. Not so smart, though, to be wasting free time on Drew Adams."

The kettle whistled, but I didn't reach for the dial to turn off the flame. The piercing sound made Riley step back. "Thanks for the advice, but I'll decide what I do with my free time. Drew's definitely not a waste of anything."

I spun the dial, turning off the flame.

Riley sucked in her cheeks. Every angle on her face looked sharper, harsher. "Oh, Lauren. You're still so new. I just hope you're able to keep up now that you've added a boy to your list of activities."

This conversation needed to end. *Now.*

"Thanks for the concern, but I've got it." I poured steaming water in a blue mug, ripped open a packet of white tea with raspberry, and poured in a packet of Splenda. "Enjoy your movie."

I turned away from the stove, leaving Riley standing there. I shot Clare a quick smile on my way to the door.

"'Night, Lauren," Riley called. "Just remember that you can't drop every advanced class when things get tough."

I almost stopped midstep, anger rising inside me. Riley had hit my sore spot, and she knew it. Gritting my teeth, I forced myself to keep walking and not turn around. I stomped down the hallway, trying not to spill my tea, and pushed open my door.

"*What* is her problem?!" I asked no one. I put my tea on my nightstand and just stood there, rubbing my scalp. *She's jealous about Drew,* I told myself. I'd known this, and Khloe and Lex had pointed it out to me. But no matter what was going on with Drew, that didn't make it okay for Riley to go after me about grades.

I sat on my bed, trying to get my mind clear of Riley and onto homework, but I knew it was useless. A serious vent session was needed.

I dialed Brielle, crossing my fingers that she would be home.

"Laaauren!" she answered.

"B! Hi!" I said. "Omigod, hi! You're home—yay!"

Brielle laughed and I heard a muffled sound through the phone. It sounded like she'd shut her door. "I'm grounded for tonight," she said. "So ridic. Mom and Dad got mad about a C that I got in English. A *C*."

I made a sympathetic sound. "Sorry. When do you get released from jail?"

"Not until Monday! Monday! I had all of these plans and now I have to stay home all weekend. Mom and Dad totally took the grade way too far. The C was *just* in homework. Not like it was a midterm grade or something." Brielle groaned.

"I wish I was there," I said. "Ana and I would sneak in and hang out with you." I laughed. "Remember that time you were grounded and Ana and I came inside through the back door? Your mom came into your room and—"

"You dove under my bed and Ana jumped in my closet," Brielle finished, laughing. "I had to look at my mom with a straight face and tell her she must have heard me talking to myself."

"At least you get to use your phone," I said.

"I had to call Tay—" Brielle stopped midword. "Oh, Lauren. I'm sorry. I didn't mean to say that; it just came out."

"You can talk about Taylor," I said. "We're still friends. Why did you have to call him?"

"He was picking up Ana and me to go to the movies with him and a bunch of people from our class. I had to let him know that his dad could drive right past my house—no movie for me."

It was a little weird to hear Brielle talk about Taylor. My old friends were going on with their social lives and their activities at Yates. I was still grasping the life-didn't-stop-because-I-left concept.

"I'm sorry you couldn't go," I said. "But I *am* glad we're getting to talk. You'll get your English grade up— no worries."

"Can I FedEx you my homework sheets for help?" Brielle asked.

"Sure. I'll add them to the top of my homework mountain," I teased.

"What's going on at Canterwood?" Brielle asked. "Anything amazing?"

I smiled. "Yeah, actually. Something really amazing. I cut class for the first time ever today."

There was silence on the end. "Who are you?" Brielle whispered. "Put the real Lauren Towers on the phone or I'm dialing nine-one-one!"

We giggled. "It was an accident!" I protested. "I was on a lunch . . . *date*, I think, with a guy. Drew."

"Laurbell! You're dating? OMG! Does Ana know? Does Taylor? When did you start seeing this guy? Tell me everything!"

I settled back onto my bed, propping my head against my cushy pillows. "I'm not dating, exactly. His name is Drew Adams and he's a rider. And a swimmer, too, which is kind of crazy. But he's not at all tan like Taylor. He's got this perfect pale skin, black hair that's kind of medium length and wavy, and the bluest eyes I've ever seen."

"You have the bluest eyes of all time," Brielle said.

"He's got me beat," I said. "Mine are light blue. His are this intense ocean blue. He's *très* cute and he asked me to lunch today."

"Where?"

I smiled at the thought. I loved telling Brielle about Drew. At home, she'd been my go-to girl for everything boy related. I closed my eyes, pretending for a second that I was on my bed at home and Brielle was minutes away.

"He asked me to The Sweet Shoppe—the café that I sent you and Ana pics of," I said.

"Oh, right! The blue-and-white place in your Canterwood photo album on FaceSpace."

"That's it. He invited me during our lunch period and I had the *best* time."

I told Brielle what we'd talked about, how easy the conversation between us had been, and what Drew had ordered for us.

"It almost was poetic that you missed French," Bri said, laughing. "That's the sign of a really good guy that he got what you liked."

"I think so too," I said. I twisted the drawstring on my plaid orange-and-red pajama shorts. "I struggled with liking him. I had to think a lot about it, and my new friends helped convince me that it was a good idea to let myself like him."

"What do you mean?" Brielle asked. "Were you sticking to your original no-boys plan to focus on school and riding?"

I took a sip of tea.

"At first. Then it kind of morphed into me feeling guilty about dating. I was with Taylor for five months. I know we had all summer to adjust to breaking up, but it felt, I don't know." I paused. "Like I was cheating on him or something."

"Of course you're not," Brielle said. "You guys are friends and he'd want you to be happy. I'm *so* excited for you and Drew. Remember that you're not with Taylor, and let yourself like Drew or whoever you want."

"Thanks, Bri. It helps to hear that from you. What about *you*? Any boys?"

"Nah," Bri said. "And if I keep getting grounded there never will be!"

I giggled. "You'll find a guy. You always do. Talk to me next week and we'll see what your status is then."

We talked for a few more minutes, then Brielle had to hang up. I checked to be sure I hadn't missed any BBMs from Khloe and put down my phone. Talking to Brielle had calmed me down from my earlier altercation with Riley, and I settled into homework, waiting for Khloe to come back.

Our door opened just as I finished a science worksheet. I jumped off my bed, staring at Khloe, who stood in the doorframe. Her eyes met mine, and it felt as though we held our breaths at the same time.

"Khlo?" I said.

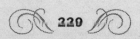

"Itwasthebestdateever!" Khloe screeched, racing toward me. She grabbed me in a hug, almost knocking me over.

"Omigod! I knew it! Yaaay!" I hugged her back.

"He was *so* great! Oh, my God, Lauren. I even forgot to check my teeth after dinner because I was having so much fun." Khloe hung up her purse and kicked off her shoes.

"Ahhh! Tell me!"

I shut our door and sat on Khloe's bed next to her.

"We ordered pepperoni and mushroom pizza," Khloe said. "At first, I kept wiping my mouth after every bite and being extra careful not to get sauce on my clothes. Zack was being neat too, but he was *eating*. After my first slice, I relaxed. We talked about classes and stuff we like to do in our free time—he loves doing anything outdoors—and he asked lots of questions about me."

"That's such a great sign!"

Khloe's cheeks got flushed as she talked. "He actually listened to my answers and remembered what I told him. We talked for so long that we almost missed the beginning of the movie."

"Who ended up picking?" I asked.

"We both did," Khloe said, smiling. "There was a comedy we both wanted to see. Zack got us giant Cokes and lots of candy."

Khloe held up her left hand. "He held *this* hand during the movie!"

I laughed. "Khlo, that's so cool! You better not wash it."

She laughed. "Never. The movie was really funny and we laughed a lot. After it was over, he walked me back and took my hand. He asked if I wanted to go out again."

"And?"

"I said yes! Obviously!" Khloe had never looked this happy.

"I'm so excited for you! It sounds like the *perfect* date. You did great, just like I knew you would."

Khloe shook her head. "You kept me as calm as possible before he got here. I probably would have canceled at the last minute because I was scared."

"No, you would have gone. But maybe your nails wouldn't have been as pretty."

We smiled at each other.

"I'm glad you had fun, but I'm *also* happy you're back."

Khloe got up, rummaging through her pajama drawer. "Lonely without me?"

"Very," I said. "Want to watch a movie?"

Khloe nodded, changing into green capri-length sleep pants and an oversize white T-shirt with a faded

CANTERWOOD CREST ACADEMY logo on the back. I put my books away. Tomorrow would be busy at the stable, and practicing for the show was only going to get more intense. But right now, all I wanted to do was watch a movie with Khloe.

25

IOU

SUNLIGHT STREAMED INTO OUR OPEN BLINDS on Saturday morning. Khloe and I had slept in, and she'd just gone to get us tea from the common room.

"Here you go," Khloe said, putting a steaming mug in front of me. "Think of me like your personal assistant all weekend. I owe you big-time for everything you did for me yesterday."

"No way," I said. "Thank you for the tea, but like I said yesterday, I did that stuff because you're my friend. You would have done the same."

"I would have. You're right." Khloe smiled. "So, does that mean I don't have to drop off your laundry bag like I was going to?"

The look in her eye made me laugh. "Hmm. No, you *can* do that. But just that one thing."

Giggling, we sipped our tea, each of us sitting on our unmade beds.

"I'm so glad it's the weekend," Khloe said. "Is there anything we *have* to do?"

"I have some homework, but that's it. I was thinking about riding in a little bit."

Khloe looked out the window. "It looks beautiful out. Riding sounds perfect. The schooling show isn't that far off, and Ever and I have some work to do."

I took a sip of tea, nodding. "Same. Whisper and I have a lot of things to work on. Dressage needs work, for sure, but I'll have to take her out on the trails for the trail-riding class. Or make up my own obstacles. Wisp and I haven't done enough trail riding for me to know *everything* that would spook her."

A look—I couldn't tell what it was—passed over Khloe's face. She parted her lips as if she wanted to say something.

"We had some rough transitions during a recent dressage lesson," I continued. "Also, I want to make sure we don't ignore jumping, even though I'm not showing in that class."

"I'm sure you'll be fine," Khloe said, looking at me like I'd spoken French. "You won't have any trouble with a schooling show. Not with your past."

"I haven't shown in a *long* time. Never with Whisper." Khloe had to understand that I wasn't the rider with titles that she'd seen on TV. She knew how hard I'd worked to get where I was and how there was *no* way I'd ever feel calm about the upcoming show. "Still want to ride with me and help with a couple of things?"

Khloe nodded. "Sure. Of course I do. People should be coming to *you* for help, though!" She smiled at me.

My laptop, open on my desk, rang. For a half second, I debated about ignoring it and talking more to Khloe, but I got up to answer the Skype call. Showing was a sensitive topic and I was probably projecting my feelings onto Khloe.

I hurried to answer when I saw Becca's icon.

"Hey, little sis!" Becca said, her face popping up on my screen.

"Hey!" I said, sitting down so my face was in view of the camera. "What're you doing up this early on the weekend?"

Becs stuck out her tongue. "I got up at eleven, thank you very much. I'm meeting some friends at the mall in a couple of hours. Mom said I had to get up and wash Dad's car before I went."

"Ha," I said. "Remember when you used to pay me to do that for you?"

Becca shot me an *I'm your older sister* look. "Yes, Lauren. I do. But without you here, I've got more money to spend at the mall today!"

We laughed. Becca's shoulder-length brown hair was pulled into a ponytail and she had a skinny pale-pink headband holding back the new bangs she'd gotten. I was so happy to see my sister. It felt like she was in my room.

"Since you're not washing Dad's car, what are you doing?" Becca asked.

"Riding Whisper soon," I said. "We've got to practice for the schooling show that I told you about."

"That'll be fun. Oooh!_Speaking of things coming up, have you started planning for your favorite day of the year?"

I shook my head. "Too busy. But I will soon."

"Laaauren. October thirty-first is not just Halloween. It also happens to be your birthday. Your *thirteenth* birthday!" Becca was inches away from the camera, getting more and more excited.

"Lauren!" I looked away from the computer at Khloe.

She put down her phone. "Sorry to interrupt, but your birthday is on Halloween? And you didn't tell me?! Um, say hello to your official party planner!"

"Introduce me to this party planner," Becca said.

I looked back at the screen, laughing. "You guys! Okay." I picked up the laptop and faced it toward Khloe. "Becca, this is my new bestie and roomie, Khloe. Khlo, this is my sister Becca."

"I'm going to throw Lauren a killer party," Khloe said to Becca. "Don't worry."

"I'm not," Becca said. "Lauren's told me a lot about you and I know you'll make it an awesome day. You know what, Lauren really likes—"

"And that's enough," I said, giggling.

"Hey!" Khloe and Becca protested.

"You," I said, pointing to Becca, "Skyped *me*. And you"—I turned to Khloe—"shouldn't let Becca give you ideas. You'll wake up to find your inbox full one morning if you do."

"E-mail me!" Khloe shouted, looking around me, trying to see the camera.

"I totally will!" Becca called back.

"Do I have to separate you two?" I asked, laughing. Khloe made a *poor me!* face and Becca shook her head. Becs and I went back to talking, with Khloe interjecting whenever she could. Finally, I ended up bringing the computer onto Khloe's bed, and the three of us talked. As much as I'd teased them earlier, I couldn't have been happier that my roomie and my sister got along.

26

NOT-SO-PRIVATE
PRACTICE

A COUPLE OF HOURS LATER, KHLOE AND I HAD
the horses tacked and were warming them up in the big
outdoor arena. Khloe hadn't made another comment about
my preparedness for the schooling show. I chalked up what
she said earlier to a misunderstanding. We'd agreed to
warm up, then work on dressage and finally trail riding. It
worked out well that we'd signed up for the same classes.

Beneath me, Whisper yanked her head against the reins
and crab stepped. She was full of energy since there hadn't
been a lesson yesterday. I pressed my boots firmly against
her sides, moving her forward. I couldn't be distracted for
a second today.

Ahead of us, Khloe trotted Ever in a serpentine. The
bay mare's strides were even and smooth. Khloe was going

to knock out the competition at the schooling show. I was unfamiliar with the riders at area schools, but I knew Khloe. Riders like her didn't come in second.

I closed my fingers around the reins and sat deep in the saddle. Whisper had to settle down before we got to work. If she kept this up, all of her energy would be wasted on the warm-up and she'd have nothing left for a serious practice. I focused every ounce of energy on her—making sure each part of my body was in agreement and signaling her to ease up. After lapping our half of the arena twice, Whisper's ears stopped flicking back and forth. She flicked one back to me, listening, and kept the other forward. She stopped fighting me to go after Ever, who was cantering in a graceful circle, silky black tail streaming behind her.

"Good girl," I said. I gave Wisp an inch of rein, tightening my calves against her sides. She moved into the free trot I asked for, and soon we'd worked up to a canter. Whisper's long strides rhythmically pounded the soft dirt, and I glanced over in Khloe's direction to see what she was working on.

Khloe had eased Ever to a walk, patting the bay's neck. The Hanoverian blinked, looking sleepy in the sunlight.

My tailbone bounced against the seat, and I straightened my head, feeling Whisper's once smooth canter start to get bumpy. She knew the second that I wasn't paying attention. I didn't want to halt on a bad note, so I got her canter back to its smooth, easy gait by the time we reached the halfway point of the arena. I asked Whisper to keep cantering along the wooden fence, bypassing Ever, and not slowing to a trot until I asked for it strides later. We shifted to a walk and I circled her so we walked toward Khloe and Ever.

Whisper was younger and much less experienced than Ever. I knew it now, and I'd known Whisper didn't have a strong showing background when I'd gotten her over the summer. I didn't want to hold her to Ever's standards, but it was going to be hard not to. Khloe's mare moved exactly as I hoped Whisper would someday.

"She had some pent-up energy," I said. I halted Wisp and she reached her muzzle toward Ever. The two horses sniffed each other, reacquainting, and Khloe and I smiled at them. It was impossible not to.

"She looked a little jerky through some gaits, but you got her under control pretty fast," Khloe said. "Wisp is such a nice mover."

Even though what Khloe had said about Whisper's problem was true, it made me defensive anyway. "We've got a lot to work on before the show," I said. "But I think Wisp has come really far since we started here." I kept the edge out of my voice as it threatened to break through on my last words. Khloe and I were riding together to call each other on problem areas and give constructive criticism. I couldn't be a poor sport about it.

"So," I said, wanting to hurry past what I'd just said, "what do you want to work on first? Dressage or trail?"

Khloe leaned back and swatted a horsefly off Ever's shoulder. "Dressage sound good? Then maybe do some exercises for trail class, like opening and closing the gate, then going out to the field? I want to go back to the stable and grab the fly spray before we go. I sprayed Ever, but the flies are getting her."

I made a sad face at Ever. "Bad flies," I said. "Dressage sounds perfect."

"Got any exercises in mind?" Khloe asked. "We can help each other on specific areas."

"Hmm. I'd like to work on engaging Whisper's hind-quarters and improving her balance."

Khloe nodded. "Okay. Let's add bending and straightening exercises to that."

"I love it. We've got four areas to work on. That seems like enough to me." Whisper, agreeing with me, let out a tiny snort. Ever snorted back, causing Khloe and me to start giggling.

"I don't think they're as excited to work as we are," Khloe said, shaking her head at Ever.

We decided to work on bending first, to loosen up the horses, and took separate spaces in the arena.

"Serpentines from a walk through a canter?" Khloe called. "And we yell out if we need help or if we see a mistake the other isn't correcting?"

"Let's do it!" I said back.

I took a breath, sitting deep. I wanted Khloe's feedback, but at the same time I hoped there wouldn't be reason for too much of it. Part of me wanted to show Khloe the side of me she hadn't seen—a rider who'd competed all over the country. A rider who wanted to get that back.

I guided Whisper through an easy serpentine at a free walk. I kept the first one large, not causing her body to bend as much. When I made the pattern smaller, she stretched through her neck and back. Glancing over, I looked at Khloe and Ever. Khloe had Ever walking through a smaller serpentine, and the mare's body twisted and bent at beautiful angles.

I tightened the reins and took Whisper through a serpentine as tight as Khloe and Ever's. Whisper didn't have any trouble, so I let out the reins and asked her to trot. We were halfway through the exercise when hoof beats sped up. Whisper turned, and Khloe trotted Ever through a tight serpentine.

"Khlo," I called. "Ever's losing balance through the middle."

Khloe nodded, her black helmet bobbing. "Right! Thanks!"

I eased Whisper to a walk, letting her take a breath before we shifted to cantering. It was as if Whisper wanted to perform well. *It's not a competition,* I reminded myself. *It's practice.*

"Laur," Khloe said. She'd halted Whisper. "I noticed that Wisp looked like she was rushing through the last serpentine."

"You're probably right," I said. "I didn't catch it."

"Maybe start her again at that pace and then begin cantering?" Khloe suggested.

"Good idea." We looked at each other for a second. What *was* this? Did Khloe feel the same way—that this was *not* practice? It felt like a two-girl show.

I turned Whisper away from Ever, mad at myself. This was the side of myself that I'd displayed when I'd ridden for Double Aces, and I hated it. I'd turned everything into a competition and couldn't take critiques from other riders. Khloe was my best friend at Canterwood, and I had to stop making it seem as though she was pointing out faults where there weren't any. She was listening to my suggestions, and it was only fair that I did the same.

Whisper and I started the exercise as Khloe had suggested and I realized, halfway through, that Khloe had been right. Whisper trotted faster than necessary and her trot became bumpy. I did a half halt and she responded, slowing. Her trotting evened out and we finished the serpentine.

"Thanks for pointing that out," I called to Khloe.

She smiled and we kept working. We moved through stretching, balance, and engaging exercises. With each exercise, we traded critiques more and more often.

I jerked up my head when I noticed someone sitting on the top fence board at the end of the arena. Khloe noticed at the same time.

"What are you doing?" I called to Riley. She was dressed to ride in black breeches, boots, and a crimson scoop-neck tee.

The dark-haired girl raised her hands, palms up, as Khloe and I approached her. "Just watching," Riley said. "I thought I'd pick up some tips from you two."

"It's kind of a *private* practice," Khloe said. "You mind?"

Riley smiled, resting her hands on the fence. "I won't interrupt—promise. I don't think there's a stable rule about me watching. Or did Mr. Conner add one and I missed it?"

I felt a heat wave of anger radiate off Khloe. "Fine. Stay there. Next time, bring a notepad."

Khloe wheeled Ever around and I followed on Whisper.

"She's ridiculous!" Khloe hissed when we were strides away from Riley.

"It's all on purpose. Riley wants us to stop so we don't get in more practice time. Let's keep going and pretend she's not there. Like, she's a giant horsefly that you sprayed away."

Khloe giggled. "I like that image. A *giant*, pesky fly with black hair." Her brown eyes looked determined. "Leg yields?"

I waved my arm. "You first. We'll change it up. One person is instructor, the other is the student. Then we'll switch."

Khloe moved Ever a few strides away from Whisper and me. I watched, calling out suggestions, as Khloe worked through leg yields with Ever. She started with simple leg yields, then progressed to leg yields along the wall and then on the diagonal. Finally, Khloe halted her mare. "Your turn," she said.

"You guys were great," I said. "Ever kept her body so straight—it's beautiful to watch."

Khloe smiled. "Thanks."

I pushed Riley out of my mind, not wanting her to make me nervous, and asked Whisper to move sideways, keeping her body straight and parallel to the long side of the arena. She responded, moving easily. We did the exercise a few times in both directions, and when we started leg yielding along the wall, sweat ran down my back. I was concentrating so hard.

I started Whisper at a walk and after a few strides asked her to keep moving forward but also sideways, ever so slightly, at the same time.

"Get her to flex her head a little the other way," Khloe said. "She's looking in the direction she's going."

I chewed my lip, starting over. Whisper moved correctly for a few strides before shifting her head in the wrong direction, throwing off our movement. I tried to keep Whisper moving forward and correct her at the same time.

"Her head's off again," Khloe called.

I nodded and, after another try, got Whisper to

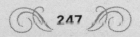

perform the movement correctly. It took every bit of training I had to get her through the movements. We finished and I let out a giant breath, turning Whisper back to face Khloe.

"You're doing so well with her," Khloe said. "She's going to be a great dressage horse."

"Girls, *come on*." Riley hopped off the fence and walked between our horses, stopping. "Aren't you best friends?"

"Yeah," Khloe and I said at the same time.

I glared down at Riley. *What* was she doing? Riley reached up to pet Whisper's cheek and I almost wanted to swat her hand away.

"Whoa, so defensive," Riley said, crossing her arms and leaving Whisper alone. "I'm just trying to help in this *situation*."

"What are you talking about?" Khloe asked. She didn't even try to keep the annoyance out of her voice.

"Khloe, it's natural that you don't want to see it. Or acknowledge what's going on. Don't feel bad. Maybe you genuinely *don't* realize what's happening."

I shook my head, dropping the knotted reins around Whisper's neck. "What, exactly, is 'going on'?"

Riley made a *you poor thing* smile. "This 'practice' session seemed more harmful than helpful. You both rode against each other the entire time. Arena battle, much? You kept checking to see who was doing what and who performed what move better." Riley laughed. "No wonder your horses were confused."

Khloe and I were silent. Birds twittered in trees lining the woods. They sounded as if they had bullhorns.

Riley stroked Ever's black muzzle. "Khloe, you have to deal with the fact that even though Lauren is on the intermediate team, she's an advanced rider. You saw it for yourself on the DVD."

My mouth opened, but nothing came out. Khloe's entire body went rigid.

"And Lauren." Riley looked up at me. "At least I'm not so jealous and intimidated by my roommate's riding that I'm trying to outdo her in everything."

I wanted to shout at Riley that she was wrong, but I couldn't speak.

Riley shifted her gaze between both of us. "The whole time *you* both have been focused on each other, I've been working on *my* riding and classes. That's why I'm doing better than both of you. In *everything*."

What Riley said sped through my brain. It wasn't true about Khloe. I wasn't jealous of her—not like the way Riley made it sound. But when I thought about our last lesson, Riley had been *on*. Her practices had been better than anyone's in our class. Even Lexa's.

"You are *so* wrong," Khloe snapped. Her cheeks flushed an angry red. "I can't believe you're standing there saying that."

Ever's and Whisper's ears swiveled at Khloe's tone.

"Aren't you embarrassed?" I asked Riley, jumping in. "You have no idea what's going on with Khloe and me, but you just stated all of these 'facts' that aren't even close to the truth."

Riley didn't move. "Well, if you're both *so* in agreement that I'm wrong, then I must be mistaken. I stepped in as a concerned teammate, but if neither of you see any validity in anything I said, I'll leave you to practice."

"Leaving's a good idea," Khloe said. She seemed seconds away from dismounting and speaking to Riley at a face-to-face level.

With an airy wave, Riley exited the arena. I played with Whisper's mane and heard Khloe taking deep breaths. Finally we looked at each other.

"Did that really just happen?" I asked.

"I wish I could say *no*. I really, *really* don't like that girl," Khloe said. "She's trying to shake things up before the show. Too bad we are *friends* and she doesn't have any pull over us like she thinks."

"You're right. We're not jealous or insecure about our riding with each other. My past is that—my *past*. I came to you for help. Today, we're helping each other. Would we ride together if we didn't want the other to do better?"

Khloe shook her head, then smiled. "The only thing Riley got right was that we're best friends."

27

KHLOE-LESS

NEXT WEEK STARTED WITHOUT INCIDENT. Khloe and I fell into a comfortable routine of school, riding, and making time for fun at the end of the night. Drew and I texted a few times every day and each time I saw him, I got embarrassingly giggly. I kept hoping that would stop soon. Like, yesterday.

I walked back from Hawthorne after glee practice, humming a song we'd just run through. It was finally midweek, and all I could think about was the upcoming weekend. This weekend was *definitely* not going to be like the last. After The Riley Encounter, Khloe and I had kept practicing in the arena. There hadn't been an ounce of weirdness while we prepped for our trail classes. The good vibes between us had carried through the rest of the weekend. We'd met up with Lexa, Cole, and Jill for a movie.

When I'd last seen Khloe at lunch, we'd had a major gossip fest with Lexa and Jill about Riley's trip to New York City this weekend. Clare and Riley had been absent from lunch. Riley had probably dragged Clare off to run lines.

I reached my room and went straight for my bed, dropping my bag, kicking off my shoes, and stretching out. Maybe Khloe would be up for a common-room study session tonight. I typed a BBM and sent it to her.

Lauren:

KK, want 2 study in cm rom 2nite? Lots of snacks. ☺

I'd changed and spread out my homework when my phone beeped.

Khloe:

SO sry!! 4got 2 tell u I'm going 2 sleepover 2nite. Be back in the am b4 class!

I stared at the message. Where was Khloe sleeping over? It *definitely* wasn't at Clare's, because Riley was there. Lexa and Jill's? Hurt settled over me. Khloe and Lexa had a friendship separate from mine with them and as a group. I was *completely* fine with that. But when was Khloe going to tell me that she wasn't coming to our room tonight? Before she went to sleep?

I wrote back.

Lauren:

OK. C u 2mrw.

I turned off my phone.

28

THIS ENDS
NOW

THE NEXT MORNING, I WAS UP AND OUT OF my room insanely early. I'd set my alarm so I'd be gone before Khloe got back. I'd been so confused about last night that I'd left some homework to do this morning and had watched mindless TV most of the night. I'd thought about blogging or even updating my neglected Chatter, but I hadn't been in the mood. I knew it was childish to duck Khloe, but I didn't care.

I turned on my phone as I walked toward the library. There were only a few junk e-mails—nothing from Khloe.

Inside the deserted library, I found a desk in the back and got to work. Riley's words from Saturday started playing in my head. *"So jealous and intimidated . . ."* I jammed ear buds in my ears. Riley wasn't going to be right—I wasn't about to focus on Khloe and let riding and school fall apart. Khloe would find me and explain about the sleepover. There *had* to be a rational explanation for last night.

But what if there's not? What if Khloe didn't want to sleep in our room last night?

Ugh. I cranked my music louder, inching up the volume until all of the questions floating around my brain unanswered were drowned out by instruments and melodic voices.

By the time I got to the stable, I still hadn't had The Conversation with Khloe yet. I'd seen her in English, where she'd apologized for missing me this morning. After that, nothing. She never told me where she'd been, nor did she apologize again.

Not that I'd given her much time—I'd walked into English just seconds before Mr. Davidson entered the classroom. The same went for every other class Khloe and I shared.

I did BBM Khloe before lunch, telling her not to wait for me, because I was grabbing a sandwich and finishing homework outside of the cafeteria.

Khloe had written back a sad face and said she'd see me

at the stable. She hadn't asked where I was or if I wanted company. For the entire lunch period, I'd sat outside on the science building steps, munching on a turkey and rye sandwich. Lexa had texted me, saying she was sorry I was stuck with homework during lunch. I wrote back and told her I'd catch her at the stable.

I walked into the tack room, looking for Lexa. I had to ask her about last night. If Khloe was keeping something from me. If anyone would know, Lexa would. Then I'd have something to go on when I did talk to Khloe.

". . . but what about during class?" A girl's voice—Khloe's voice—came from the tack room. I stopped just as my hand reached to push open the door.

"What do you mean?" This voice was deeper. *Drew.*

"Mr. Conner doesn't treat Lauren any different, does he?" Khloe asked. "With her background, I—"

She wasn't even trying to be quiet. Anyone could hear Khloe questioning my position in class. I spun away from the door, tears making it hard to see as I ran down the aisle. Everything I'd worried about was true. *Riley* had been right. Khloe thought I got some sort of special treatment during lessons because of my past competition experience.

"Lauren! Geez!"

I looked up, a step away from smacking into Lexa.

"Why are you running? Mr. Conner's going to—" She stopped, her brown eyes going over my face. "Lauren. What's wrong? Omigosh. Why are you upset?" Lexa's voice was so gentle and comforting.

"Khloe!" Her name burst out of my mouth. "I know she slept over with you last night because she probably doesn't want to be my roommate anymore. The DVD ruined everything! Things are weird between Khloe and me."

"Laur—"

"All of these little things have been happening and I kept brushing them off," I said, interrupting Lexa. I swiped my hand across my nose. "But Khloe really does have a problem with me. She's in the tack room right now talking to Drew and—"

"Stop!" Lexa shouted. The horse in the stall next to us jerked his chestnut head back, snorting.

I froze. I'd never heard Lexa yell. Lexa inhaled through her nose, looking straight at me.

"Go to the hayloft," Lexa said. "Stay there. I'll tell Mr. Conner you weren't feeling well."

"I can't miss my lesson," I said.

Lexa put her hands on her hips. "Do you really think you'll have a good session right now, the way you feel?"

I shook my head. She was right. I'd mess up Whisper if I tried to get through practice like this.

"Go. Right now. I'll be up in a minute."

I didn't argue again. I walked down the aisle, checked to make sure Mr. Conner wasn't around, and pulled down the wooden ladder. I'd never used it, but the loft seemed like a good place to hide.

I sat down on a wooden pallet, resting my back against a hay bale. There were stacked high, and it felt like a fort. I dropped my head into my hands. *You'll talk to Lexa and figure out what to do,* I said to myself. *Lexa will be here in a minute and you'll find a way to fix this.*

Boots shuffled against the ladder. Lexa walked around a stack of hay bales, stopping in front of me. Her posture had relaxed and her gaze was calm.

"Mr. Conner was cool about your lesson," Lexa said. "And Khloe's."

"Khloe's?"

Khloe emerged from the same spot where Lexa had appeared. I'd been so focused on Lexa, I hadn't even heard Khloe.

"Sit," Lexa told her. Her tone was firm, but caring at the same time.

Khloe looked at her, shaking her head, but sat across

from me on another pallet. We gazed at each other. Khloe looked confused.

"What's going on?" I asked. "Lex, what are you doing?"

"Clueless here, too," Khloe said. "Why am I up here? And Lauren, you look like you were crying!"

I didn't respond.

Lexa walked over, standing between Khloe and me. "You guys are my closest friends. I love you to death. Really, I do. You're both good people and your friendship is too important to *me* and to both of you to be damaged or ruined."

Khloe's expression was blank. "Ruined? By what?"

"By you sleeping at Lexa's to get out of our room and by you asking Drew if I got special treatment during lessons!" I said. "How could you do that?"

Khloe's head jerked back, her cheeks flushing. "*What?* I did *not*—"

Lexa held up a hand, stopping her. "*That* is why you're both up here. Some communication needs to happen. Whatever you guys have going on needs to be worked out. Clearly, neither of you are talking to each other about the biggest problem here—jealousy."

Khloe and I looked at each other. We didn't say a word.

"You guys are going to be up here a *long* time, then,"

Lexa said. "Don't either of you tell me you're not jealous in some way of the other. Or have wondered if the other person feels that way about you. You've both come to me and said the same thing."

I sagged against the hay bale. Khloe looked like the air had been knocked out of her.

"I'm not saying either of you has talked about the other in a malicious way, because you haven't," Lexa said, softly. "I am saying you've worried about what the other person is thinking, and you've repeatedly come to me to see if I know. We're all friends. Coming to me instead of talking to each other stops now."

Lexa stepped back. "I'm going to my lesson. Don't come down until you've talked. Please."

She turned and disappeared behind the bales of hay. The sound of her boots on the ladder rungs lessened with each step down she took, and soon she was gone.

Khloe and I were alone. I played with a piece of hay, twisting and breaking it into tiny pieces. I glanced up at Khloe, and she was doing the same. This couldn't be *it*. My friendship with Khloe couldn't be over before it even had a good chance to get started.

Had Khloe been acting the whole time? If so, what did that mean for our friendship? I couldn't believe we were sitting across from each other in the loft. We'd had such a communication breakdown that Lexa had needed to corral us so we'd talk.

But I didn't know how we were going to move past the Drew thing. She'd talked to the boy I *liked* about me. I couldn't sit here all afternoon and not say anything. No way was I leaving, either. Lexa was right—this cycle had to stop.

I looked at Khloe. Her eyes met mine. They were fiery—like the day Riley had confronted us in the arena. She sat up straighter, dropping a twisted piece of hay.

"Guess we have some things to talk about," Khloe said, her voice flat.

"Yeah, looks like we do."

ABOUT THE AUTHOR

Twenty-five-year-old Jess Burkhart (a.k.a. Jess Ashley) writes from Brooklyn, New York. She's obsessed with sparkly things, lip gloss, and TV. She loves hanging with her bestie, watching too much TV, and shopping for all things Hello Kitty. Learn more about Jess at www.jessicaburkhart.com. Find everything Canterwood Crest at www.canterwoodcrest.com.

New girls.
Same academy.
And some serious drama.

Join the team at the Canterwood Crest Academy at

CanterwoodCrest.com

Illustration © Glass Slipper Webdesign

Only the best class schedule, ever!

- Watch the latest book trailers
- Take a quiz! Which Canterwood Crest girl are you?
- Download an avatar of your fave character
- Check out the author's vlogs (video blogs)!